Sacred Minds & Sunlit Souls

SHELEILA D'PAIVA

A catalogue record for this
work is available from the
National Library of Australia

National Library of Australia Catalogue-in-Publication data:
Sacred Minds & Sunlit Souls /Sheleila D'Paiva

ISBN:
(Paperback)

ISBN:
(Ebook)

To everyone on this never-ending journey of growth, I see you xx

Recap

Katelyn had always dreamed of travelling, but the notion had always felt distant with the demands of her job, her relationship and societal expectations of what she should be doing at her age. Get married? Have kids? Career progression? Or take a leap of faith?

Katelyn takes the leap of faith, first setting foot alone in Reykjavik, Iceland. She begins to reinvent herself in this new world of adventure. She continues to England, Scotland – where she reunites with estranged family – and ends up in Hawaii, leaving her boyfriend and starting a new life without the familiarity of home.

1

Thrive

"And tilt your head back a little bit more, Naomi," I yelled to the bride. I watched as she tilted it back, a smile spread so enthusiastically across her face that I was mesmerized by the creases around her mouth and eyes. I know women prefer them edited out, but I liked to keep them there. It looked like happiness to me, those moments in pure joy that you don't care about how the world sees you because you are so present in your body and how that moment feels to you. The rest of the bridal party posed in unison, naturally tilting their head back a little more, laughter filling the space around us, mixed with the sound of the waves crashing in the background, the birds chirping.

It was a perfect October's day in Oahu, the sun was shining and I was surrounded by sand and water, doing what I loved. I had called Oahu home for nearly a year now and had grown my photography business locally with the help of John and his art studio and its rapport within the community. Couples were booking me for their weddings on different islands and I was booked for the next six months. I could hardly believe it.

Naomi, from London, had been in touch after seeing my work posted on Instagram and changed her wedding date so I could be her photographer for her wedding here, something I didn't take for granted, or lightly. It made me want to make their day as special as it could be. I had been up since four am while her and her bridesmaids were getting ready, dancing to Michael Bolton (I didn't ask questions) while sipping on cold mimosas. I had a feeling we would actually be friends after this. One of those people I could call in a years' time, say I'm in London and she would make time for me. One of those kinds of people. There was something about her, the way we connected instantly, maybe because I shared my experiences of being in London last year. Not just her though, but her bridesmaids too. Her and her soon-to-be husband were celebrating their twenty-year anniversary with their wedding. I liked that. I liked that it wasn't another date they had to remember, and it worked out perfectly, us trying to navigate the dates. It was intimate, forty people or so. Their closest friends, and you could feel it.

She had planned the day beautifully, starting with a ceremony on the beach. There was a small floral arrangement on a frame nestled into the sand, a perfect arrangement with the ocean in the distance and a small marquee with servers handing out champagne. It was a strict two hours of photos with absolutely everyone – family, the bridal party, guests. She even made sure I was in a few too. That was followed by limousine pick-ups for everyone to the local Lorita Hotel – a five-star hotel with a beautiful outdoor courtyard, surrounded by greenery and secluded for privacy. Everyone danced, drank and as my shift was finishing in the evening, I took a seat with some cake, pondering how different my life looked now, reminiscing how I used to stare out at a sea of grey buildings. I never knew so much could change in twelve months.

I wondered if this would happen for me. *Would I ever get married? Would I find the guy of my dreams?* I was in my mid-thirties now, single and one of the few of my friends who hasn't been married and doesn't have children. The only messed up but somewhat silver lining, a bronze lining potentially, was that I had noticed some had started going through separations now. *At least I wasn't in that bucket?* Or maybe this wasn't the path for me in this lifetime. Maybe, this is my life now. Maybe, it's travelling and loving what I do and how I do it so deeply.

Naomi and her husband were dancing together, the sun had set but the warm light globes surrounding them were making their side profiles burn golden. I stood up to take some more pictures, to capture the way they looked into each other's eyes with an infinite amount of love and gratitude. It had been twenty years. I had seen this look when people were getting married in their first five years, ten years even. But, twenty years? This wasn't a young or new love. This had been the result of experiencing an entire life together and still choosing each other.

"What's the secret?" I asked them when the song had finished. I asked everyone this, trying to find patterns. They looked at each other and laughed, he nodded at her to speak. I noticed that too, the way the men liked hearing their wife's version of the story.

"The little things," she said, not breaking her gaze on him, "picking a best friend, the one you laugh the most with," she continued on.

"I mean, I just knew when I saw her," he said, "there is nothing I wouldn't do to make her life better." That had been the pattern I had found – the little things.

2

Beginning

After the hike with John to Diamond Head last year, we spent the rest of the day discussing the terms and conditions of the art gallery and moving into his place. He spent a few weeks training me up and showing me how his business ran. We discussed how I could incorporate my prints into the gallery and what I could – and couldn't – use to showcase them, and we discussed how we would connect remotely while he was away. When I think back to it now, I don't know how I instantly trusted him, but I did. The only due diligence I did was stalking him on social media, visiting his gallery and chatting to locals about him. Everyone knew him – mostly as the bachelor he was, but also because of how involved he was with the community.

He stayed for Christmas and New Year, something I hadn't truly considered while I was swept up in the move, taking me to parties and introducing me to people. When the festivities finally quietened down into January, we formally signed a contract and he left for Portugal. That's when the new reality of my life hit me. The world began to slow down as I had begun a new routine, the adrenaline that had been coursing through my veins since I had quit my job and booked that first flight to Iceland began to disappear. The heightened experiences I'd been chasing fell away and the realization that I didn't have my close friends, little income, a sore heart and absolutely no idea what I was doing with my life or the new direction I was going in finally hit me. Besides work, I stopped doing anything and meeting anyone – and I even started to miss Mark. It wasn't because of a lack of people around me or things I could do, but finally processing the loss of my old life, finally grieving it. I was exhausted from so much change within such a short period of time it had finally caught up with me – emotionally, mentally and even physically. Repeating the same story again and again to someone new, the effort of getting to know new people all the time and everywhere I walked still feeling unfamiliar to me, *Maybe it was all too much too soon? Maybe I hadn't thought this all through.*

I knew Mark wouldn't instigate a conversation with me, but I felt ready to call him. If nothing else, I knew we needed to discuss what was happening with Luna, all my things in our house and all that we shared together.

"I'll just buy it all from you," Mark said when I asked him what he wanted to do with our apartment. I couldn't hear any emotion; he didn't tell me how he was feeling. We managed to get stuck straight into it.

"Sure. And it makes sense I take Luna given your work schedule," I'd responded. He agreed. I told him to pack my things in boxes, which he said he'd already started, and drop them to Mom's place, along with Luna, whenever he was ready.

"Does that mean you are coming back?" he asked, but I fell silent. I didn't know. I knew it was good to hear his voice again, to feel someone familiar, even though we were only talking about how we were dividing our assets and organizing arrangements for our little fur baby girl.

"I don't know, I will stay here a little longer. John said he will be in Portugal for about a month. I'll arrange for Mom to fly Luna over to me or I'll try and visit next month and pick her up myself. I haven't figured it out just yet." It was the truth at least. I knew Mark had more questions to ask, but I didn't have any answers. I had no interest in knowing if he was with anyone or what he was doing but there was still a comfort talking on the phone with him. We spoke for an hour about nothing deep, until the conversation had nowhere else to go and we both knew we were done.

I didn't end up going back to Manhattan though, Mom thankfully loved looking after Luna. It allowed Mom and me to Facetime often, so our relationship grew stronger. She became my best friend, and even though I knew she enjoyed our regular chats, she was constantly telling me I needed to get off the phone with her and start meeting people.

While John's original plan was to only travel around Portugal for a month, I had begun using my finance skills to grow his business and allow it to run more efficiently. I had automated systems, implemented a marketing strategy and outsourced work – his business was growing, he was very pleased with me and the work I was doing, which was also reflected in my pay increase, and yet I had more spare time. His month in Portugal suddenly turned into a world tour but he would always check in with me every few weeks to see if I needed anything and how I was managing.

"I'm going to start a photography business," I said to him one check-in about four months later, after Mom had been hounding me to do more with the time I had. He was thrilled.

"If I can help you in any way, please ask. This is a great move, I'm so proud of you," he quickly responded. I realized that John had become a father figure to me. Well, what I thought one should have been – supportive, kind and present. There was never a call of mine he didn't pick up or an email he wouldn't get back to quickly. He sent me contacts and introductory emails to help with the business, anything he thought of on a whim to support me, he would do.

From selling my prints through his gallery, I began offering people discounted photoshoots around Hawaii. This naturally meant making myself visible again. I started posting on social media every day and slowly but surely activity increased, along with bookings. It grew quickly. As did the assumption from everyone else, that life was and had been … perfect.

3

Space

As the days followed, I posted pictures from the wedding, tagging as many people as I could and sharing as many things as I could to my stories. I was changing hashtags and creating quick Reels. I noticed many brides appreciated something – anything – sooner rather than later. Usually I outsourced this, but this wedding felt extra special to me, because of Naomi, and I wanted to do it myself. I know she would have appreciated that.

Not long until mine, my best friend Adeline commented on one of the Reels.

I can't wait, I responded, a part of me feeling guilty because if I was being honest with myself, I could wait – I wasn't looking forward to heading back to New York.

Dan proposed to Adeline shortly after Mark and I broke up. She had flown to Oahu for a few days in January after John left, partly because I think she knew I was struggling and partly to tell me face-to-face before she shared it on social media. When I saw her at the airport, I instantaneously burst into tears. I ran to her, crying. We hugged and laughed and cried at the same time people around us looked and smiled as we embraced each other for what would have seemed like an eternity, which only felt deeper when I saw the diamond on her finger and realized what else she needed to tell me. I took her around to all my favorite places, but most of the time, we sat at home and drank the Australian wine she brought back for me and chatted in John's lounge room. She wasn't here for Hawaii, she was here for me. She told me how she'd thought Dan was going to propose on their holiday in Australia, and how he did it in one of the wineries in the Hunter Valley, when they decided to travel around Australia to see some of his family.

"I didn't know whether I should tell you," she said, honestly, with difficulty. It hurt my heart that my best friend didn't know if she could tell me something she was so excited about.

"Please don't ever not share something exciting because of what I'm experiencing," I said to her truthfully, "my heart can be breaking for me but be full for you." And both were true at the time.

Her engagement was now coming up, which I had already told her I couldn't make, but I would dial in somehow.

"Don't be silly, close the gallery and go," John said multiple times.

"She's your best friend," Mom said each time we spoke.

"I totally understand how you feel, babe, you do whatever you need to do. I love you no matter what," is the response Adeline gave. And this is why I loved her so much. She knew it wasn't that I didn't want to be there for her, but because I wasn't ready to face everyone and everything else. *What if people asked me questions about it?* I heard Mark had started dating a woman in his office, a direct message through Instagram that I hated waking up to one morning. While I know Adeline wouldn't be inviting Mark, it didn't make the questions I knew I would get any less intimidating.

Adie's engagement party was a month away now, an entire year on the waitlist to the venue they wanted. When I thought about going though, I got little pangs of pain, almost a sickish feeling in the pit of my stomach. I didn't know if it was guilt or anxiety – probably a mix of both. I knew I should be flying back to be there for her, but continued to justify it with whatever excuse I could come up with.

"You know you can stay with me, right? It won't cost you a thing besides the flight." Adeline voicemailed one day, after I told her I loved the pink flowers instead of the blue ones she sent me the photo of … and that I was devastated I wouldn't be there to see it in real life. *Maybe she was using reverse psychology on me, a slow burn while I helped her plan the day?*

"I know, I just can't, babe," I responded, but each time I said it, it didn't feel any more true.

While my bond with Adeline and my mom grew, most others slowly rescinded. My cousin Alice included. Maybe because of the different time zones between Edinburgh and Hawaii, or maybe because we began relying heavily on social media instead. We would like and comment on stories and posts with only the occasional DM to check in, then the voice notes and calls disappeared. Uncle Pat, however, would send me WhatsApp messages every now and then. He wanted to know where I was, who I was with and what I was doing. While he was a man of very few words, the care he took with me to make sure I was okay was beautiful. He really did feel like my uncle now.

"Do you need any money?" he would ask. No-one had ever asked if I needed money since I left home. Not that I would have ever taken it, but he made me feel like my support network had gotten so much bigger, even though he wasn't physically with me or that we spoke often. I would randomly get pictures he found of me or the family or share little stories as they came up. I loved that about him, the effort, the little acts he did to let me know he was thinking of me. It was all I needed. I think it's also because he knew a little bit about how I felt – leaving home and settling down somewhere new. The dynamic of loneliness through all the excitement. *Was it all worth it?*

4

Therapy

As fulfilling as the last year had been, it had also been a struggle.

You're so lucky, Kat, everyone would write on my posts, *You're living the dream,* they would say, my heart aching each time. While I know my social media showed the highlight reels of my life, I felt no-one understood just how much it felt like my life had burnt to the ground and the sacrifices, pain and fear I went through from having to start from scratch. I think John knew, and that was the likely reason he would also check in with me so often. I think there was a sense of responsibility on his part for meeting me when he did and somewhat being a catalyst for that final straw at the bar, the night Mark decided to leave.

"I think it's about time you stop moping," John would say on the phone to me every time I told him I had no other plans outside of the art gallery that weekend, "I want you to go see my therapist please."

"I'm fine, I'm just busy," I would say. He knew I wasn't busy.

I've paid for your first session. It's booked for tomorrow ten am. Close the art gallery for an hour and go to it, he texted me one Tuesday afternoon. It was three pm, and I was sitting on the couch watching *Selling Sunsets* on Netflix. I noticed my first reaction was annoyance. *Who does he think he is?* I was about to respond with those exact words, but after a few moments decided to instead let him know I wasn't going. Then, as I looked, at the black screen on the TV asking *are you still there?* in white letters, I caught my reflection. I looked drained, my messy ponytail loosely drooping to the side. I decided to at least try it out once, to get John off my back. One session.

The therapist wasn't far from John's apartment, it was a ten-minute walk and I thought it was best to get some sunshine and exercise. I felt nervous, not knowing how it would work or what they would ask me. *Was I supposed to prepare for it? Did I need to write down talking points?*

The building was a small beige one, covered in greenery. There was a small sign with their logo on it, reading 'Mindful Therapy', with a website and phone number beneath it. There was a small bell that rang when I opened the door, and the receptionist, who looked to be writing something in a notepad, promptly looked up at me and instinctively straightened her back and smiled. She had blue eyes and dark brown hair, neatly parted in the middle. She was wearing a white shirt and a brown cardigan, one of those fuzzy ones that always reminded me of sheep skin.

"Ah. Hi. I'm Katelyn. John booked this session for me. I think it's with Dr Lin," I responded, quietly, shyly, approaching her desk with caution. The receptionist nodded her head, told me to take a seat and picked up the phone, mumbling something I wasn't quite able to pick up.

"Katelyn?" a woman called from another archway, past the receptionist. She looked Vietnamese, a little taller than me, maybe mid-forties. She was dressed modestly but had a soft look about her, that kind glisten that some people had which naturally made you feel comfortable with them. I stood up from my seat and followed in the direction she was walking until she stopped and gestured me into a room around another corner. The room was homely. To the right side of the room there was a green couch with a wooden table to the left of it, a tissue box, bottle of water and matching glassware neatly perched on it. To the right of the room, there was a wooden desk covered in papers and files, pens and notes. Dr

Lin closed the door and ushered me to sit on the couch. I watched her push the chair under the desk and walk to another single-person green couch in front of the longer one where I sat. I looked around the room, taking in the sights and the smells. It smelled like lavender. I didn't know if this was on purpose or if it was the scent of Dr Lin. The walls had large paintings throughout, with the only bare wall being the one behind me, with a clock.

"It's so lovely to meet you, Katelyn," she said, to begin. "John has told me all the amazing things about you." I smiled, nervously. I didn't know what to say, so she went on. "He told me you have just moved here from New York and were starting a photography business, how is that going for you?"

"It's going well," I responded.

"Do you like it in Oahu?"

"I do, I love it," I said. I could feel the tension slowly move away from my body, relieved she hadn't asked me any difficult questions. I naturally started thinking about all the things I loved about being here.

"What do you love most about it?" she asked, like she was reading my mind.

"I love the ocean and the weather. I find it's relaxed here, so laid back, but also so much to do."

"That's right, it's funny how both things can be true. It's my favorite thing too. I love the sunsets here. I go with my family a lot," she said. I looked over to her desk again where there were paintings on pieces of A4 paper, something her child must have done for her. There was a photo on the desk too, it looked to be her, her husband and a little boy.

"Have you been here all your life?" I asked.

"I was born here, but my husband and I have lived and studied abroad before. We have both lived in the UK and Canada. We actually met in Canada, but we wanted to settle down back here, for the reasons you just mentioned actually." I nodded again, not knowing where to go from there.

"So, why do you think John booked this session for you?" she pressed on. I shrugged.

"He thinks I'm wasting my time here, I guess," I said. I felt like I was answering her like an annoyed teenager, but the truth was … no words were actually coming to me. It's like my brain had frozen and I could only speak the bare minimum.

"And, do you agree with him?" she asked me.

"Yes … no … I don't know," I began saying; she didn't say anything. "I've probably felt a little bit out of my depth. I know he wants me to leave the house and go do things but it's like I've lost my energy," I said. "I'm not depressed though," I quickly added.

"I don't blame you for losing your energy, moving countries is a big deal. It's one of those big life changes that knocks your nervous system. Everything is new. New people, new ways of doing things, even new weather. You are adapting and it takes a lot more energy than we realize," she said. I quickly felt comfortable, like she was on my side. I hadn't thought of it like that. "Are you starting to feel lonely though?" she asked. I nodded. "And is there anything proactive you have been doing?"

"I think it's the thought of explaining to people why I'm here that overwhelms me. I don't think I'm ready to talk about breaking up with my ex and moving here on a whim with no plan. It seems like so much drama," I said, almost with a hint of shame. My face flushed, and I know Dr Lin saw it too.

"You don't need to share things with people if you don't feel ready to. Why not shift perspectives – that you're embracing life in a new city, and you want to explore and meet people? Maybe you don't need to mention the break-up at all. Just say you visited here and loved it and decided to see where opportunities take you?" she said. I remained quiet, realizing the negative story I had been telling myself. *Did I think I was a burden on people? Was I embarrassed that I was a thirty-five-year-old single woman now working casual hours in an art gallery earning less than half of what I was in New York?*

"I wouldn't even know how to meet people. All my friends from New York are from school. I've kept to myself since being with Mark, and that was eight years of my life. I learned how to talk to people when I travel, but I don't know how to do it in an everyday setting I guess," I said. I could feel panic slightly pulse through my body. I was scared. *Why was I scared?* I realized I hadn't really needed to make friends outside of my core friend group when I was with Mark. He was a safety net. We had our life and that's all I thought I needed. *How do I even create a new life?* I sensed Dr Lin knew I was having a moment. She remained quiet and gave me some time.

"There are apps you can use to meet friends now," she shared. She started writing down different areas in Honolulu where there were people my age. She suggested meet up groups, Bumble BFF and to also join different local activities to meet people with the same interests. "What's something you enjoy doing?"

"Photography?" I responded, as she went on to share that it may be a great way to get more involved in the photography world here, meet new friends and even get me more comfortable with the business. This set us on the path of setting goals and a plan for the lifestyle I wanted. Dr Lin and I even talked about my first memory of photography, how Mom always said I should have become a photographer, but Mark didn't see it as a real job. How it was the reason I met Mark, and ultimately part of the reason it ended.

"Before your next session only if you would like another session of course," she said smiling, both of us knowing there was so much more to unpack, "if you could come in with the following answers: how do you visualize your life in the next twelve months – your work life, your hobbies, friendships and even your romantic life. We can unpack any feelings and thoughts that come to you when doing this when you come in. Today was a nice introduction, to get to know each other more and see if we are a good fit. And, Katelyn," she said, "you're experiencing a very big life change. I hope you're giving yourself credit for making some really hard decisions." I didn't know what to say. I sat in her large lounge room looking office, looking at the dark grey carpet, tracing my eyes past where she was sitting back to her desk, this time admiring a large green plant. I was looking everywhere, but at her.

"Thank you, Dr Lin. I wasn't expecting this. When can I book to see you next?"

"There is a misconception that these sessions are only for people with trauma, but we can all benefit from a safe space to talk that will give us tools and clarity, from a grounded and unbiased perspective. I see a psychologist too. We all need coaches in different aspects of our life," she responded, so gently, before booking in the same day and time the following month.

"I guess John is going to have to deal with me opening the shop an hour later every month now," I joked, as I left her office and began the walk to the gallery, a slight spring in my step, downloading Bumble BFF curiously … *How did I want my life to look?*

5

Bumble BFF

"Yes, from Manhattan but decided on a sea change," I shared with a stranger for the fourth time that week.

I had taken Dr Lin's advice and downloaded an app to make friends. Bumble allowed you to go between dating, networking and friendship. There were a few moments where curiosity got the better of me and I moved to the dating section, swiping left and right but never planning on taking it any further than that.

Mark and I had been together for eight years, long before any apps were a thing. We would meet people through going out to bars or through friends. It seemed to be different now. People felt intwined in their circles, but if these apps had so many people on them … *why was it so difficult to connect?* The thought of meeting a guy on an app to go on a date seemed foreign and somewhat contradictory, when surely they were out and about with friends doing things too. *Why couldn't we talk to each other in the bars like we used to?*

I didn't really know how to navigate the app and there were moments of anxiety. *Could I be catfished trying to find female friends? If I swiped left, is their profile gone forever or does it come back? Will these strangers kidnap me?* I filtered out people that smoked and did drugs and swiped right on women that looked like they liked to travel, read or were looking to expand their friendship circle because all their friends had kids now. My profile had that I'd recently moved to Oahu and was looking for someone to hike and explore bars and restaurants with. I had a sweaty and smiling photo of me at the top of Diamond Head with John, the ocean meeting the city in the background. I had another cuddling Luna in our once cosy home in Manhattan. I had one picture of me drinking a spicy margarita at my favorite local bar, called Hideout, in the open-aired area surrounded by green plants in terracotta pots. I had a picture of me and Adeline from Eva's hens' last year, everyone in a line by the iconic Niagara Falls. I shared my interests in art, wine, travelling and photography, feeling it was a great summary of who I was and hoped it would attract someone similar.

Most people looked friendly enough, but I did find myself growing judgemental. Some looked too nerdy, some looked too hippy and some looked too pretty. I didn't feel inclined to swipe right if they had too many tattoos or piercings, nor if they had an overwhelming amount of botox and had designer clothes on. *Was I missing out on meeting great people?*

The three friend dates I did go on were okay, but it didn't feel like they were genuine connections. One kept talking about places she'd travelled to the whole time. I didn't get a word in. Her profile was consistent with her though; she was tall and German, with long blonde hair. Her pictures were of her surfing, having beers and photos from her adventures around the world. The second date was a local, who was looking for friends without kids as she was the only one in her friendship circle without them. Her profile was wholesome. She had images with her dog outside and by the beach. When we met though, she seemed to only want to talk about EDM music and shared stories of her abusive ex boyfriends and different times she took MDMA. The last date was an influencer from the UK. She was lovely but wanted to take multiple photos, recorded some of our conversation and asked the waitress to take a video of us fake laughing. It was exhausting. It was too much, and I decided to go on one last date before taking a few weeks break and focusing on the business instead.

"I've always wanted to come here," she said, as we met for the first time at Hideout. Selina was Portuguese and had moved to Hawaii two years ago. She had this curly, dark brown hair that shined red in the sun. Her honey brown eyes, with specs of green, reminded me of Felicity somehow. I liked that we both seemed to like strong mai tais. Selina, or Sel, as I quickly felt comfortable calling her, was gorgeous, always laughing with an absurdly loud laugh that made me feel lighter. I felt an ease with her.

"How was your last Bumble BFF date?" she asked with her rhythmic Portuguese accent. I rolled my eyes.

"Do you know Carly Walker?" I said, taking a sip. Sel snorted and covered her mouth, making sure she didn't waste a drip of her mai tai.

"Oh, yes. I've caught up with her a few times. This is a small place."

"I couldn't deal with all the videos and pictures, it's not me. She seemed so lovely though," I said, sadly, thinking back to the fun we did have.

"I know, I thought I would get used to it too. I secretly liked all the photos she took as it always made for good posts, but I actually found it exhausting and began wondering if our friendship was just for the camera," she agreed. "I don't know how they do it for such a long time, surely they get over it too?" We both pondered it for a moment, in silence. I noticed that quickly about us, that we could sit in silence without the constant need to fill the space.

We went from a weekly catchup to chatting every day through one app or another. She didn't live far from me and worked centrally at the local hostel. Her background was in finance as well, but she struggled to get work in the field, given her overseas qualifications, though I never heard her complain once that it wasn't what she wanted to do. She seemed like the kind of person who would always be grateful or could find the silver lining in her situation, no matter how difficult it got. She was a breath of fresh air, even in a place as fresh as Hawaii.

She shared with me how she came to Hawaii with her now ex-boyfriend. They broke up a few months in because he wanted to go back to Portugal and she didn't. It reminded me of Quella and her love for Iceland, a reminder that sometimes places just draw people in. It's just the way it is. *Were they always just meant to be there?* It was nice to find someone in the same time in their life – single and figuring it out.

Sel shared some of her dating stories as we continued drinking, and three more mai tais in, I had switched my profile from BFF to dating again as we began swiping right, our night continuing full of stories and laughter. *Maybe John and Dr Lin knew what they were talking about?*

6

Real

I was surprisingly excited when it came time to see Dr Lin again. I had done my homework and was ready to chat about my upcoming goals. I had written it all down and felt prepared for the session.

"How are you feeling?" she asked when I sat down, my face gleaming, excited.

"Good, I downloaded Bumble like you suggested and met a great friend. I've written down everything you asked as well," I responded, eagerly, likely surprising her too.

"Sure, let's get into it then." I could tell she probably had other questions to ask, but she was going with the flow. I pulled out a piece of paper I had written everything on.

"I guess I want to start with work life, as I do really want that to remain consistent," I responded. "I want to build a big photography business, but then move toward managing it and having really great photographers work for me, that would give me some flexibility with work and life," I said.

"I like that idea, and what would you like your life to look like?" she enquired.

"I mean, if I had kids or a partner, then I could travel more."

"Do you want kids and a partner?" she pressed.

"Yes, I think one day I do," I said, the pace in my responses slowing. I thought I was more prepared for the session than I seemed to be.

"And do you think you want to do that here in Hawaii, or would you like to do that in Manhattan? Or somewhere else even?" she asked. There was a part of me that knew she had directed me here purposely.

"I don't know. I like it here in Hawaii," I said, but stopped, "but I wouldn't want to have kids without my family and friends around."

"Lots of people move with their partner overseas or interstate. They build new traditions and support networks," she said. I heard what she was saying but it didn't resonate with me. I felt like she was challenging my response.

"I don't want to do that though," I said, looking away, thinking. She nodded, writing things down.

"What keeps you in Hawaii then?" she asked softly, changing the tone of her voice and slowing the speed down. *What was keeping me here?*

"I think I have just gone with the flow since Mark and I broke up, and I hadn't really thought that much about the future and where I was going. The business picked up and I thought, great – I'll just keep doing this … and now here I am." I watched her write more things down. This session was getting deeper than I had planned.

"To clarify, you haven't done anything wrong. I'm just curious," she said sweetly. "I think you did a good thing giving yourself time alone, to experience living somewhere else and making new friends. I think it was beautiful you put so much trust in John and the relationship you have cultivated with him."

"John's great. I feel he's like the father I never had. Or uncle. He's so kind and helpful," I said instinctively. Dr Lin smiled, nodding her head slightly while writing more, agreeing with me but not saying anything else.

"Close your eyes for a second," she asked. I closed them. "Take a breath, feel your body from your head to your toes, take another breath. Now, how do you feel when you think of moving back home?" I waited a moment, a felt a pang of something.

"Scared. Or, maybe … embarrassed?"

"Shame?" she asked. *Shame?*

"What do you think you're embarrassed about?" I could feel my sinuses start burning, and I was actively holding tears back as best I could. I thought for a moment. The words came flying out.

"The thought of going back and facing everyone's judgement, or sympathy, or advice. It exhausts me thinking about it. And a part of me feels like it's my fault the relationship didn't work, like there is something wrong with me. And that I'm so behind again. I am living at a random person's house who I barely know, making barely any money. I sold my share of the house to Mark and I just don't have anything." It all came out, with a vengeance. Stories I didn't even consciously know were there. There was no holding anything back, even if I tried. I realized it wasn't Hawaii I wanted, it was Manhattan I was scared of. "I'm staying here because I'm scared of going back." I finally said, after the silence and two scrunched tissues in my hand, my body heavily breathing to get oxygen in. *Was I having a panic attack?* Dr Lin walked toward the table closest to me and poured me a glass of water to take a sip.

"I want you to know, all these emotions you are feeling are valid and normal," she said kindly walking back to her chair. "I do feel we need to reframe your mind. Our mind is our most powerful tool. Yes, it will be hard when you go back, there will be questions and judgement, but you have to be confident in who you are and why it needed to happen," she said, her voice soft and stable. Her words flowed gently and perfectly paced. I had never thought I was running away from anything, but it's like a switch flicked inside of me. I nodded and looked at her, but the tears hadn't made her come into focus yet, her silhouette blurry. "I would like you to start writing down affirmations, of what you would like your life to look and feel like. Write it in present tense. You can do a line for each one, or you can do multiple lines, whatever you would like to do. Start with, I am healthy, happy and whole or I make the right decisions based on my values. Anything to summarize who and what you are."

We discussed the importance of affirmations a little more, but as I calmed down, I needed to move toward something less heavy. Dr Lin knew how eagerly I wanted to talk about the rest.

"Okay, sure, go for it – tell me about your ideal man then," she laughed.

"Brown eyes, dark hair, athletic, six-foot," I began, thinking of the men I swiped right on over the last few days with Sel. Dr Lin let me finish, with a face I couldn't read.

"Why don't we focus on what kind of person he is and how he makes you feel, shall we?"

"It's a given though, they have to be kind and funny and treat me well," I said.

"Okay, I hear you. And is this the list you have used in the past then? Was your ex, ah – Mark – kind, and funny and treated you well?" she asked, circling what I think was Mark's name on her notepad. I regretted pivoting to men instantly and wanted to go back to the safety of friendships and business.

"I mean, kind of. When I first met him, I thought he was all those things. I put him on a pedestal. I thought he was everything. Over time, he just got so busy with work, and we had stopped doing things together," I said, realizing I had started to justify our relationship.

"So, consistent effort is important to you?" she asked. I nodded. "Write down those things, the values, the little things they do and the kind of person they are. Remember, looks fade. The spark isn't necessarily an indicator the relationship has potential. Sometimes it's an unconscious response that the person reminds you of a past attachment figure who hurt you. Think about the essence of someone."

I looked at the time on my phone and saw it had nearly been an hour.

"That went so quickly," I said, as she laughed, "and started much differently than I had planned."

"You can't plan these things, that's the beauty of it. We will get wherever we need to go with it, and I think we made some great progress today. You will likely process some information about being here and moving back to Manhattan. See what comes up for you and write it all down and we can chat about it next week," she said. I nodded in agreeance, and held myself back from hugging her, even though I wanted to. *Where does this leave me now? Would I really move back to Manhattan?*

7

Decisions

"Essentially you're running away from facing your problems?" Sel asked bluntly, after I shared my second psychologist appointment with her. She had this kind way of being brutally honest and not shying away from difficult conversations. I could see she was asking it in a way she could understand, while she took a sip from her fresh mai tai the server had placed on our table. We were back at our local, the Hideout, and had been there so much together over the last month the servers would make us one without even asking,

"I mean, I didn't think I was before the session. I thought I was just trying something new and enjoying my life here," I said to her, contemplating her question but also not sure if I was being truly honest with myself.

"Both can be true though. You could have been, but now you're avoiding it?" she asked; I agreed. "Why don't you go to your friend's engagement party? You haven't been home for nearly a year now. The longer you leave it the harder it might be to go. Maybe this is a great opportunity to test what comes up," she said honestly. I didn't know what to say. An inkling within me made me feel it was true, that maybe I did need to go back, sort out those boxes at Mom's place, and see Luna again. "Would you need to see Mark again?" Sel asked.

"I don't think so. We sorted the house out quite quickly and he transferred me money for the furniture, so unless it was about Luna, I don't think there is anything else," I said. After calling Mark when I felt homesick in the beginning, he called me back a month later and apologized for leaving Hawaii so abruptly. I knew there were moments of weakness for each of us, but we knew in the deep core of us we were incompatible. It was during that conversation we discussed the house, that he would buy me out, knowing I didn't have the funds anymore. I remember the feeling of that phone call, it was surreal. I felt it was the official end of eight years together. An end to the relationship with the man I thought I was going to marry and have children with. To a life in Manhattan, where our apartment was in the same building as a pizza shop that reminded me of my home in Brooklyn. To a life with our Luna and each other. While I know it wasn't a waste, it was still difficult to process and let go. To allow us both to let it go.

"Is there anything I can do to help around the art gallery, if you go?" Sel asked. I pondered, swirling the straw in my drink, my mind doing the same.

"I'll call John soon. He said I could close the gallery and go already, but I don't know if he just expected me to fly for the wedding, not the engagement. Maybe I will go for a few days and see how I feel?" *Is it time to go back again? Is it time to see everyone again? Am I ready to create a new life back home?* I knew how special it would be to be there for Adeline and my family. The more I thought about it, the more the resistance naturally fell away. I could feel myself leaning into the idea.

"You have to go on those dates before you leave though," Sel added, the fries being placed on our table between us, our mai tais halfway down the glass. The sun was setting in front of us, we watched it kiss the horizon and then slowly melt away, taking all my reservations with it. I took a breath, relaxing my shoulders on the exhale.

"Do I have to?" I joked, trying to perk up at the thought of dating, "Go on those dates I mean?" Picking up three salty, warm fries and feeling the soft potato melt in my mouth.

"Yes, entertain me. I want you to have all the fun and share all the stories. You haven't locked anything in?" she asked.

I shook my head sideways, "Let's do it now." I unlocked my phone, opened the only dating app I used and handed it to her as I watched her scroll through the men I was talking to.

"Why do I need to be the one that suggests the time and day though?" I complain.

"What do you mean? This Tom guy asked you about tomorrow six pm at The Grill and you haven't responded." I rolled my eyes playfully, remembering that I thought Tom was cute when I first read it but put it in my 'too hard' basket. "So, guess where you're heading tomorrow night to see him." She threw my phone back at me, a cheeky grin spreading across her face, already responding to Tom that I was looking forward to it. He gave it a thumbs up with a winky face emoji.

"You're secretly trying to keep me here, aren't you?" I teased, throwing a single fry at her, secretly glad she pushed me to get out of my comfort zone.

"I just want you to feel you truly gave this place everything before you leave, men included," she winked, picking the fry from the table and eating it. *I guess I could continue to entertain Sel, what have I really got to lose?*

8

John

It was a slow Thursday evening when the front door of the gallery burst open and startled me. It was unusual for that kind of energy, especially so close to closing time, that I physically jumped. He stood there, a big smile and gusto oozing out of him, his linen white shirt with the two top buttons undone and matching styled beige linen plants. The man who had travelled the world in the last year, his eyes full of stories and his body covered in a terrible tan.

"John?" I asked, as his great big smile could see he surprised me, "What are you doing here?"

John usually kept me up to date with his travel plans, or generally checked-in every couple of days to see how the gallery was going and if I had any questions. It had been like that for the entire time, but as I was busy figuring out … my life … I had forgotten to check in with him, even though I had told Sel I would reach out to him soon.

"I'm back!" he exclaimed. My mind moving faster than my body as I got up from the seat to give him a hug, it slowly registering he was in front of me after such a long time.

"But why? What happened? Why didn't you tell me?" I know I sounded concerned and looked bewildered.

"It was time, Kat. I kind of had a moment and realized this gallery may also be the reason you are putting your life on hold. I'm sorry it took me this long."

"Four weeks surely did escalate," I joked. He laughed. Thankfully. "I'm sorry I haven't been able to get your place ready for you though, it's probably a bit of a mess." John didn't mind, he was chilled like that. He quickly dived straight in and filled me in on how he had just come back from India, where he was doing an ayurvedic retreat in Kerala.

"Twenty-one days of vegetarian meals near the jungle. It was wild, we were drinking ghee to purge every day, getting treatments. I feel like a new man. It was there I had the thought of coming back home, like someone else was telling me. It felt right. I just knew." John had already shared with me how difficult it was to find permanent staff. He couldn't go away for long periods of time as staff would leave or they needed more management, sometimes coming back to messy accounts or stolen pieces of art.

"That sounds amazing, John, but honestly, it's fine. I've loved it here and been able to build my photography business," I said, "and I haven't paid for accommodation for a year now. So really I'm still thanking you." While I assumed John was a wealthy guy, I never knew how wealthy or wanted to take advantage, but he always insisted he didn't want money from me and was happy to pay me for my time at the gallery as well. I was the one who felt he drew the short stick. *But how wild he came back at the same time I was experiencing the need to go home?*

"You know what that means, right?" he asked. I looked confused. I didn't. "It means, you can go home if you want now. I've got it covered here," he said.

"Have you been talking to Dr Lin?" I asked cheekily. He laughed, shaking his head.

"Oh, enjoying the sessions, are you?" he said with a big grin. "Your conversations are safe with her, but I've been in therapy for long enough to know that you need to go home." He knew all too well that I needed it too. "When's your friend's engagement party?" he pushed. John wasn't the type to go off course or not get the answer he wanted.

"Next month," I began. "I've actually been meaning to call you and ask but I've been procrastinating, thinking of things I needed to do here and my photography bookings. I just don't know." I trailed off, anxiousness causing me to think back to Eva's bachelorette, when everyone was asking me about my relationship. Everyone was talking about babies and marriage, and I hated being there. *Will this be ten times worse?*

"You don't have to worry about the gallery Katie. Depending on how long you go, I'm sure it won't be a big deal to bring your photography sessions earlier or push them a bit later."

"I'm also worried about what they'll say," I said, my eyes breaking contact with him, almost embarrassed.

"Well, Dr Lin can support you with how to respond, but just say, I'm not ready to talk about it right now, or this is a conversation for another time, we are celebrating our friend today. It's called boundaries," he said with conviction. It was a pretty good idea; it was all a good idea. "Or you can tell them the truth, you have nothing to hide or be ashamed of, you have done what's best for you," he said. I was so grateful for John. From the moment we met, we just clicked. He felt like family. He was family.

"Oh, but, John, I have a date at six pm at The Grill?" I said, looking at the time. He looked even more excited.

"That's great. Why don't we close up shop now, go for a drink until six pm. I'm back now, we have plenty of time to catch up."

We closed the gallery and headed to the bar next door. It was exciting hearing more about his travel adventures and the art he saw throughout his travels and what he'd brought back. He told stories about who he met and his next plans for the gallery. Then, he asked about me. I shared how therapy was going, my realisations, meeting Sel and starting to date.

It felt bittersweet, but just like that, I knew I could feel the universe was conspiring for me to finally head back to New York. *Ask, and you shall receive, right?*

9

Learning

The change of plans created a change of pace. I found energy and excitement when the nerves had passed, likely due to finally making a decision on going back to Manhattan in the first place, no longer choosing to be in limbo. I felt I was fully embracing my time in Hawaii now. I went on more dates, some good and some bad, and felt it took the pressure out of the conversations. It felt like a month of thrills, as if I wasn't coming back, even though I was.

"So, are you planning on staying here?" Tom asked. We were at a restaurant by the water on our third date. I liked that he planned our dates. I liked that he was six foot, athletic and had a shaved head. He was ticking my boxes. He was ex-army, saw a psychologist, read books and did ice baths. He was the epitome of health to me, physically and mentally, although he made me feel the opposite because I didn't wake up at five am to lift weights or go for an evening run every day.

"I'm not sure, I am figuring it out at the moment," I responded, not having a wine because he said he didn't plan to drink that evening. I wondered if this is the kind of guy I should date. *Surely, he would make me a healthier person?* The only downside was that he constantly called me 'cute' after the first date, which felt condescending, and one evening he 'joked' that I didn't put much effort into my appearance because I decided not to wear heels. *Is this what Dr Lin meant by how someone makes you feel?* I soon found out he was dating me alongside his ex-friend. I ended things.

Then there was Talim. Talim told me on our first date that him and his wife had just separated because they were different people. He had cheated on her multiple times because she wasn't adventurous enough for him and didn't want to hurt her feelings. Of course, he wanted full transparency moving forward. I wasn't sure how I felt about that but thought there was no harm in a second date. He cooked me dinner at his house and after a few hours of him acting weird, he pulled out a plate of cocaine and asked if I wanted some. I ended things.

There was Paolo, he was South American and divorced with two children. On our first date he told me that his wife wanted to open the relationship. She ended up falling in love with the other person and they separated. He had not felt attached to the woman he was dating and didn't want to fall into another relationship trap. It was our first and only date.

Leon was an interesting character. He was from the UK and talked the entire time about himself. He ordered dips and bread for the table, then proceeded to keep it solely in front of himself and not offer me any. He told me not to worry, that he would get the wine. At the end of the date he walked me to my car and attempted to kiss me, I managed to turn my cheek in time, but the quick step back during it told him all he needed to know.

"I mean, they were all such gentlemen, I guess," I told Sel, who was unconvinced.

"Why, because they paid for dinner?" she asked, rolling her eyes, not impressed by the story after story I told her. I nodded, "Katie, that's the bare minimum of a good man."

I hadn't considered that; I didn't know how a man was supposed to treat a woman. Growing up without a father and not dating before I met Mark, I didn't know any different. *Were men supposed to pay? Would they change if they cheated? What was a real red flag?*

Thinking back to my conversation with Dr Lin, I thought about what kind of man I wanted to be with. Thinking of my dating experiences, I knew I wanted:

MONOGOMOUS, KIND, FUNNY, TRUSTWORTHY, TRANSPARENT, TRUSTS ME, MAKES ME FEEL SEXY, VALUES ME, IS MY BIGGEST FAN, GENEROUS, CARES ABOUT HIS HEALTH, GIVES ME COMPLIMENTS, SMART, DOESN'T DO DRUGS OR SMOKE, DRIVEN, I FIND ATTRACTIVE, TAKES THE LEAD, GENEROUS.

I thought about what was missing with Mark, and continued my list:

ADVENTUROUS, WANTS TO TRAVEL, PUTS IN THE EFFORT, HAS A WORK/LIFE BALANCE, WANTS TO HAVE EXPEREINCES WITH ME, PUTS ME FIRST, APPRECIATES AND LIKES MY PHOTOGRAPHY, SUPPORTIVE OF MY GOALS AND BUSINESS, WOULD NEVER JUST LEAVE ME IN A COUNTRY BY MYSELF.

With the list, I was able to clearly see why the guys I had been on dates on didn't align with me. Then I moved onto values. *What were my values, and how did I see my life?*

FREEDOM, FLEXIBILITY, GROWTH, KINDNESS, TRUSTWORTHY AND TRUSTING.

Why aren't we taught these things in school? I decided from then on, I was only going to make decisions and allow people in my life who aligned with these traits and values. Although, dating was again on the back-burner, and I was ready to shift my energy back to Manhattan.

10

Sel

The month flew by due to all the dating and the gallery getting busy, and before I knew it, it was time to head back to Manhattan. I kept my things neatly in John's spare bedroom and proactively sent boxes back to Manhattan ahead of me. A part of me was prepared to not actually come back, even though I knew I had to and thought I wanted to.

It was surreal sitting at the airport again for the first time in about twelve months. The last time I was at one, besides picking Adeline up from the airport, was when Mark and I were leaving Edinburgh for Hawaii. It brought back memories of seeing Quella for the first time talking to everyone while she waited to board. It reminded me of meeting Christian, the art distributor who complimented my photography skills on the way to London. It felt nostalgic. The airport felt like adventure and change, but it now also felt comfortable. The first time I hopped on that first flight to Iceland, I was nervous. I packed and repacked my bags. I checked my passport multiple times. I was anxious and scared and got to the airport early. I didn't know what I was doing or what to expect. This time, it felt comfortable. I wasn't nervous about packing, knowing I had everything I needed back home. I wasn't worried about getting to the airport early or how I would find the gate. There was an ease about it this time around, even though it had been some time.

Sel wanted to take me to the airport, so she picked me up from John's place.

"You're acting like you aren't coming back," John laughed as I hugged him goodbye, "my spare room is full of your stuff, so you better be back." He always knew how to make me laugh, to make light of any situation. It was him to the core. Even though I knew I was coming back, I felt like crying, a grateful and thankful one though.

"Ready?" Sel asked, as she took my suitcase from me and wheeled it to the car while I continued a drawn-out goodbye to John. Sel beeped the horn and waved at John, a reminder it was time. "You okay?" she asked as I got in the car. I nodded and appreciated that Sel understood the need for silence on the drive.

"Honestly, drop me off," I insisted, as she drove into the parking lane. She rolled her eyes as she followed the signs to short-term parking and parked anyway.

"You know, one day you need to get used to people wanting to do things for you," she said. She sounded like my therapist. It was some-thing I was trying to do, trying to accept help and not undervalue myself, but in moments like this, it was hard. *Did she know how much parking at the airport was?* She helped me with my bags and walked straight to the bar when we got inside.

"You've only got carry-on and we've got time," she said before I could discover another excuse. She could tell I was a bit uncomfortable. "It's going to be so much fun seeing everyone again, you know?" she said, reminding me of the positives of the trip.

"I know, it'll be good."

"You've done so well building a life here, Katie, please remember that and share it with people you meet. Your business is booming, you're quite literally the top photographer in Oahu and you've only been at it less than a year."

"I know, I know," I said embarrassed. It's hard talking about myself, let alone give myself credit for my work. A part of me also feels like it's gloating. *Where's the line between being proud and sharing your successes, and gloating for what you've done?*

"People who love you want to celebrate your successes with you, you know that right?" she added, like she read my mind. I nodded and took a sip of the pinot noir sitting before us, swirling the liquid around in the glass, fixating on the red vortex in the middle of it as the scents and aromas lifted and comforted me. Sel continued to ask me about my family and friends, and where I would be.

"How was Adeline when you told her you were coming?" she asked.

"Over the moon, and she quickly told me Mark wouldn't be there, which I was thankful for. I'm mentally preparing for everyone else though."

"And you're staying with your mom?" she continued.

"Just when we land to go through some of my things." Sel nodded. "Have you ever thought about going home?" I asked her.

"Never. As much as I miss my family, I've always known from a young age I wanted to leave and see the world and live somewhere else. There aren't as many opportunities in Portugal, and I love the vibe of Hawaii. There is something about it. It feels healthy, vibrant and fresh." I agreed with her. It did. It was young and vibrant. When I really thought about it, it's actually not the kind of lifestyle I wanted to live forever. I missed the city. I loved the diverse options of food or going to the latest international festival happening around town. I liked the glitz and glam, I just never made enough time to see it when I had the chance. I liked walking around the big city with Luna, and going to parks and driving through wealthy or hip suburbs. The more it came to my attention that Hawaii was not for me, the more I felt the buzz throughout my body when I thought about the possibility of moving back. Sel could tell as well. She looked at me and nudged me.

"Love you, Katie," she said, giving me a knowing look. She knew I would leave at some point. "I know Hawaii isn't for you. I can see it now. But I hope we remain friends and know I'll always be here for you." I knew the hardest part about leaving was not the city itself, but the two people that had made it home – John and Sel. The quickness in which we grew close was nothing I had experienced before. That, and the business I had built and the thought of having to start again from ground zero.

"Love you too, Sel," I said, as the text message that the flight was boarding came through and it was time to go to the gate. We hugged again, and I thanked Sel for the lift, reminding her I would see her soon. *Does leaving someone ever get any easier?*

11

Visit

The first people I saw when I exited arrivals were Adeline and Mom. Ads had made a massive **Welcome Home** sign and they were waving their hands frantically. It's something I have always loved about airports, seeing people embrace each other on arrival and families waiting in anticipation for their person to come through the automatic doors. Travelling by myself, it's definitely something I have missed. My eyes welled.

"Aw, Katie," Mom said, hugging me first, but Ads didn't want to wait. She hugged over the top of us, and I couldn't breathe, but I didn't want to breathe. My heart felt like it cracked. Like so much I had been holding together, was finally allowed to come out, to not feel I had to do it all on my own anymore, that I had my people there. I think being away from them, I forgot they were always there. That I had support. Yes, they had their own lives, but they would still be there for me even if I was on the other side of the country.

"Gosh, I really have missed you guys," I laughed through the tears of laughter and happiness.

"Come on, let's go and get you some good food and some wine, hey? You brought your coat like I reminded you, right?" Mom asked. Ads nodded, taking my bags from me even when I tried to continue pulling them along myself. The crisp winter air took me by surprise as we walked out of the airport – the smells and the sounds hitting me with nostalgia just like the cold, crisp air.

"Restaurant or mine? Or even happy to head to yours, Mrs Tallin. I don't mind the drive, or if you have space, I can stay at yours? I don't have work tomorrow."

"If you don't mind the drive, we could get there before dark and then Katie can get settled. She could head back into the city with you tomorrow?" It was settled. I did want to see Luna and get some things I needed. I was sure when Mark packed them in boxes he didn't do it in any order.

While it definitely felt like I'd been gone for some time, it didn't feel like it had been a year since I'd seen my mom, or nearly that since I had seen Ads. *Had I built this anxiety up in my head? Was I terrifying myself for no reason?* The drive to Mom's place out of the city went the fastest it had ever been as we filled each other in on things we didn't have time for in our calls, and when we settled into her lounge room, not once did they bring up anything bad. It felt good to sit there with Luna snuggled in my lap, exactly where she was meant to be. Even though we'd been FaceTiming so often, Mom and Ads wanted to hear about all the exciting things again, like the business, John and my dating escapades.

"See, mothers just know these things," she said proudly when I told her the business was making very close to what I was earning in finance. That I was booked out and how someone actually changed their wedding date so I could be the photographer. I don't know if they were purposefully focusing on the positive things, the best things about my trip, or if they didn't want to talk about the rest of it on purpose. *Did Adeline tell Mom after she visited me?*

"And who is this new bestie of yours, this Sel?" Adeline said, her eye contact breaking, jokingly trying to look intimidating by scrunching her face in disgust.

"Gosh, Ads, you would love her. She is so funny, and such a kind person. She works at the hostel close to the art gallery. She helped me get back into dating." That's the moment they both looked at each other. I guess they were holding off on purpose.

"How are you going with all that, love?" Mom asked, her voice softening, topping up my wine glass. God, it was good to drink wine with them both again.

"I know you didn't want to come back for the engagement?" Ads added in.

"I honestly was so nervous about it, Ads, but John pushed me to see a therapist and essentially, she said I wasn't facing what I needed to here. I do love Hawaii but I'm thinking it's maybe time to potentially move back home …" I began, unsure, watching their facial expressions – especially Mom's, as I hadn't told her about seeing a therapist – and also not wanting to promise them something, "… and, Ads, you've been here for me this entire time. It would have been so selfish not to be here for you on your engagement," I said. She reached across the couch and caringly squeezed her hand around my arm, the warmth spreading throughout my body even when she took it away.

"A psychologist? I did that bad a job raising you, did I?" Mom said, insecurity laced in her voice. Ads shot her a look widening her eyes. It was sweet; they almost had a mother-daughter relationship as well. Mom had watched her grow up too.

"You did a fine job raising me, Mom," I said, grasping her hand to comfort her. I was aware it's something her generation wouldn't have done, or spoke openly about, or maybe even understand due to the stigma attached to it. I felt ready to share my experience with her now.

"Dr Lin helped me understand why I stuck it out with Mark in the first place; the safety and predictability, our sessions deep-dived into my subconscious mind, and also slowly made me realize I don't want to be in Hawaii forever. It was a great experience and it's a beautiful place, but I don't want to miss all these milestones right now. She had me write down what I wanted from life, and I realized it all brought me back here. I want to build a life around my people. If my photography takes me somewhere else in time, then great. But right now, I'm living day by day in Hawaii and not working toward where I want to be and who I want to be with."

"I'm so proud of you for coming home, babe, I know it was hard for you," Ads said, as she went to take another sip from her wine glass, the tinge of red stain starting to slightly stain around her lips. I grabbed her hand to look at the ring again, the ring I had admired when she came to see me, and it looked brighter now, bigger even.

"How are you both?" I asked. Adeline started talking about the engagement planning, how things were going with Dan, as they were looking to buy a bigger place and plan for children. She told us about some drama she had at work and more about getting engaged during her Australian trip, so Mom was filled in too. Mom told us about the never-ending renovation, how they are feeling older and an update on my siblings. As they both took turns talking, filling each other in as well as me, my heart felt warm. It's exactly where I was meant to be.

12

Settled

Adeline lived in the city and decided to drive home early the next morning to get some errands done for the engagement. I was originally going to go with her, but I wanted to stay inside where it was warm and hang out with Luna. I wasn't used to the low temperatures anymore, but it was also a good excuse to go through some paperwork that Mark had left, with Mom as well. There were copies of the sale contract from the transfer into his name.

The house was officially his. I don't think I ever really stopped to think about it. That the home we built together is somewhere I wouldn't go back to. That he was now, likely, bringing other women back there. I could imagine the inside of it so vividly, where Luna used to wait for me when I got home from work, and the time she nestled by Mark's feet when he didn't get the promotion. A heaviness overwhelmed me.

I found a note in the papers. It was a letter to me, from him.

Dear Katie,

I know we've already spoken but I wanted to say it again – I'm sorry I left you in Hawaii. It's something I will always regret.

Know that I love you very much, and I wish we could have made this work.

It seems you've made your mind up though.

I've transferred you $5,000 for the furniture, given it's all dated now. If you want anything else, please give me a call and we can figure something out.

Greg quit. He couldn't stand the pressure. They finally made me partner.

Not sure when you will read this, but if you need anything, am here.

Take care,

Mark

My initial reaction was annoyance. *I had made up my mind?* But with the next breath, I felt grateful. Grateful that he wrote a note, that he transferred me the money and that there was no reason we needed to contact each other again. *Or maybe, I should?*

"Katie?" He asked, picking up the phone. We hadn't spoken since January, about ten months ago.

"Hi. I thought I would give you a call because I'm back in New York for Adeline's engagement party," I clarified.

"Oh, don't worry. I wasn't invited. Obviously, they are your friends," he said, even though he didn't need to say it. I already knew. Mark always distanced himself from my friends from the beginning anyway, always creating a distinction between who I spent my time with and who he did.

"I know, Adeline would never do that to me. I called because I got your note and I wanted to see if there was anything I needed to pick up while I'm here, although I know you would have written this like ten months ago?"

"While you're here? You're not staying?" he asked.

"I'm not sure. I just wanted to ask if there is anything I needed to do from your end? I feel like we cut the cord quite quickly and I probably buried my head in the sand a bit."

"No, everything is sorted. Is the $5,000 okay for the furniture?"

"I mean, the couch was $20,000 in itself, Mark, but let's leave it. You did me a favor by finalizing everything so quickly, so I was okay financially in Hawaii, and packed all my things up and dropped it to Mom's. I'm grateful." I wanted to acknowledge what he'd done and thank him. "How often do you get to see Luna?"

"Probably once a week, your mom's place is a bit far and I struggle with time."

"How do you feel if I take her back to Hawaii with me?" I asked out of nowhere, wondering after if I said it for a reaction as I was likely planning on moving back.

"It would be selfish of me to say no. You've always looked after her the most."

"Thanks," is all I could respond with, a calmness between us I wasn't expecting.

"Do you have enough money, is there anything I can do?" he asked.

"I'm fine Mark, thank you though."

We swapped a few more surface-level pleasantries, but the conversation naturally fizzled.

"Thanks for calling, Katie. It's great to hear your voice and that you're well."

"You too, Mark. Congratulations on making partner as well. You finally did it. I'm happy for you."

The uneasiness in the pit of my stomach during that whole conversation went away and it was probably the first time I knew, at the core of me, that this was the right decision. It felt like the closure I needed as I put the sale contract in a folder and ripped up the letter from Mark, my final curiosities at ease and an intuitive feeling that all the signs were given to me over the years, but a knowing that it was all part of my learning journey. *Did he feel the same way?*

13

Engagement

The two days at Mom's house was productive. Mark had actually done a good job putting things in boxes and sorting them categorically, so everything was easy to find. I was able to use Mom's spare car and drop everything at the Brooklyn property, a place I never thought I would be so grateful to still have.

On the second day, I took what I needed from the Brooklyn house and went to Adeline's place to get ready with her, spending time with her family and going to the venue early to help her set up. The engagement was at a rooftop bar in the middle of New York. There were large metal walls with green plants trailed across them and fairy lights somehow suspended to something I couldn't quite make out. It looked magic, with the city lights from the skyscrapers surrounding us. We were the first ones there, two hours early, checking to make sure everything was set up as planned and finalizing the flower arrangements on the tables. Adeline was wearing a full-length white fitted glittering backless dress, her hair had a perfect middle part, with loose waves effortlessly falling down her back. Dan was in a fitted beige suit. I caught a moment on camera between them after we had finished setting up. They were looking smitten into each other's eyes saying something without words, an expression of excitement and readiness.

"This is a surprise wedding, isn't it?" I interrupted them, the twinkle in their eyes saying all I needed to know. I hugged her, both of us knowing what I would have missed if I hadn't made it.

"I'm so happy you're here, bestie," she said, taking a deep breath and changing the subject to stop us both from crying. "They wouldn't return our deposit when we tried to cancel, and wanting to plan babies soon, we decided not to wait any longer. We want to just celebrate with everyone we love and focus on our next lot of goals," she responded, "and I was going to tell you sooner, but we weren't one hundred percent sure and I didn't want to force you out here if you didn't want to come." I didn't say a thing, this wasn't about me. I hugged them both as tears fell from my eyes staining my dress, understanding the care she was trying to show to me and grateful to have not missed her wedding day.

We went to the bar for a drink and some food, just the three of us, until the clock struck five pm. As the golden hour approached, the guests began arriving and I could feel my anxiety rise as the temperature dropped and people started walking towards us.

"Katttiieee, you caaaame," said literally everyone who saw me. Each time I could feel my body slightly recoil at the high-pitched voices, anticipating where the conversation may go. "You didn't post you were back on socials," was the other comment.

"Yes, the owner of the gallery I work at came back early and I was able to move around some photography sessions this week, so I was able to get some time off. It's so good to be back," I said, truthfully. Time and time again.

"How is Hawaii?"

"Have you seen Mark?"

"What happened with you two?"

"So, are you going to look for a real job?"

"Have you started dating?"

"Do you miss not having a proper job?"

The questions came as fast as I thought they would, some people being more subtle than others.

"It's great, I love it. Lonely at times without my close friends and fam."

"I spoke to him when I got back, we are fine."

"It just didn't work. It's for the best."

"I started a business instead, it's going well."

"I've dated a bit but not in a rush."

"A real job doesn't interest me when there is more money doing other things I find more enjoyable."

And even threw in a few:

"Let's talk about this another time, today is about Adeline."

"I'm not ready to get into that now, let's catch up another time."

I answered everyone one by one, giving them variations of the same response with as much enthusiasm as possible but also implemented the 'boundaries' that Dr Lin told me. It felt good to not share everything, empowering me to learn how to navigate answering questions I didn't want to answer.

"You're so lucky you travelled."

"I couldn't imagine dating again at this age … looks wild out there."

"The clock is ticking, but you didn't want kids anyway, did you?"

Then the next round of comments began as the night drew on, the worst ones of all. The ones that made me question if I did make the right decision. It wasn't luck, it was discomfort, it was change. I knew the clock was ticking, it concerned me too, no matter how many friends told me they knew people who had conceived at forty. These were the comments that were exhausting, and the reason I didn't want to come. I implemented the boundaries where I could again:

"I've worked really hard to get here, it's definitely had its moments."

"Yes, it's wild out there but it's been great meeting other people. How have you been?"

"Let's not chat about me having kids right now, how are yours though?"

Adeline made eye contact with me multiple times and saw the look in my eyes that no one else could recognize. She came up quickly and said loudly, "Katie, over here, I want to show you something," and dragged me to the opposite bar.

"You okay?" she asked concerned. "Don't worry about anyone else, okay, you've done the right thing and it's their small world and limiting beliefs, remember that." I didn't say anything except for, "G&T please," to the bartender. Ads gestured for two, and also asked for two shots of black sambuca. God, I love her, and couldn't wait to be closer to her again.

As we stood together with our drinks, we watched everyone else, almost invisibly. Until the music changed and she kissed me on the cheek. It was time for the vows. She winked at me, as my cue to get the flowers, as she stood on our side of the bar. I could see Dan on the other side, looking at her. He had seen her so many times already during the night, but this moment, as the song changed and I handed her the bouquet, I saw his eyes tear up. Mine did too.

The music started and everyone realized what was happening, hushing others and gently making a path for her to marry her groom. No one was expecting it, and a cheer erupted as they realized. Her glittering dress sparkled under the fairy lights. I didn't notice she had also attached a train to the dress during all the commotion too, and it was sparkling behind her, keeping the pathway open so people wouldn't crowd around her. The photographers and videographers running around to capture all the moments, and me, slowly following behind her, fixing her train and realizing she had even planned me being the bridesmaid without me knowing. I could tell, that right now in their worlds, everyone had disappeared to them.

I wanted that. I wanted someone to only see me. For their world to stop because that's all they saw. Them wanting to make me happy, and I wanting to make them happy.

Adeline shared during speeches that Daniel never wanted to get married, but over the years and going to other people's weddings, he saw the importance of celebrating love and combining families. She talked about all the beautiful things he did for her, all the things no-one saw, like making her tea first thing in the morning before she woke.

"I think I knew I loved him when he brought me coffee to bed the first night I stayed over. He knew it was almond milk, but not too much, and half a teaspoon of sugar. We only ordered coffee once before and I never quite got over the fact he remembered that. It was always the little things." *Always the little things?*

"And me, well, I just want to make sure she always has a smile on her face," he said. Someone, somewhere yelled 'happy wife happy life' and everyone applauded with cheer.

That. That's what I wanted. Someone so in love with making me happy. *Would I ever find that kind of love?*

14

Kiro

While I hated the interrogation at the engagement (turned wedding), there were so many beautiful memories. After the vows, they made sure everyone ate, and then half of the rooftop turned into a dancefloor. It was the most fun I'd had in over twelve months, letting loose and being around my best friend, people I had known for the longest time. I felt free. I felt like me.

Being the millennials we are, the music went from pop to house and then by nine pm it was all hip hop and R&B music, pointing to the non-existent 'windows and walls' when the words told us to. That's when I saw him. My checklist. My dark hair, dark eyes, six-foot checklist. We locked eyes and even though I looked away quickly, they were drawn back at him, who was still looking, this time giving me a quick wink.

"Who's that?" I asked Eva. Eva was pregnant with their first child, and still had not completely forgiven me for the fact I had completely missed her wedding because I'd moved to Hawaii and should have been back for it.

"Dan's best friend, Kiro," she said, "And, he's single."

Kiro had gone to the bar, and was back, now on the dancefloor dropping his arms to the beat and glimpsing my way every so often with a smile. I had never had a one-night stand before. I didn't even know if I was capable of it, but the champagne, gin and sambuca that Adeline fed me hours earlier had well and truly already kicked in and I was confident. And, I was single. For the first time in nearly a decade, I could look at other men and let loose. Something I had never done before.

We continued making eye contact until I broke it to go to the bathroom, to fix myself up and make sure I looked as hot as I felt. *Thank you G&Ts!* I then went to the bar. I scoped him out again, not being able to see him when I got back.

"I hear you're Adeline's best friend, Katelyn," he said, coming up behind me while I was in line. My heart raced, and you could cut the chemistry with a knife.

"Did your homework, did you?" I smiled, "And I hear you're Kiro, Dan's best friend?"

"And you did yours?" he responded, cheek in his eyes, not breaking eye contact. "What can I get you?"

"G&T thanks, with cucumber," I replied, not sure why I didn't say with lime. *Did I think it made me seem cooler?* He didn't even order the drink, he swished his fingers at the barman who he made eye contact with, and the barman nodded. "What was that?" I asked.

"The trick is to tip them at the beginning, they will keep serving you during the night. And lucky for you, that's what I've been drinking so I don't need to attempt to gesture for anything else."

"Where are you going after this?" I asked confidently.

"Wherever you're going," he said, watching him watch the barman, who raised his G&Ts in the air to be passed over people waiting closest to the bar.

We stayed close together for the rest of the night, dancing on the dancefloor, dancing together, and when the bride and groom left, with a quick wink at me, Kiro and I left for his hotel room, next door.

As soon as we walked through the door, he unzipped my dress. I loosened his tie and threw it across the room as I unbuttoned his shirt, unclipping his pants. He picked me up, my legs wrapping around his midsection, pushing me against the wall while we kissed and then throwing me on the bed. I watched while he pushed his pants to the ground and started kissing my knees on the way down.

It had been over a year since I had been with a man intimately like this, and a while since I had the urge to touch myself. I wondered if I even remembered how to caress a man's thickness or what I needed to do if I put it in my mouth, but as he kissed and licked me all the way to my mouth, it came back instantly.

The night was passionate, and he even woke me up a few hours later for a second round. Pressing himself into me from behind as he caressed my nipples and kissed my neck, causing waves of tingles throughout my entire body. One arm around my neck pushing my body close to his and the other hand slowly moving lower and lower until it was so moist I couldn't wait any longer. He knew it too. He flipped me around and then onto his back so I could ride him, giving me control of the speed and depth I wanted, both finishing at the same time.

I woke up before him, hoping to shower before he got up, in case he didn't look like I thought he looked, or in case he wasn't as nice the next morning.

"Can I join you?" he asked, the surprise of him walking into the bathroom and the liquid courage having worn off, I instinctively covered myself with my bare hands. He smirked, completely bare. I nodded shyly as he made his way into the shower with me, cradling the nape of my neck with his hands and pulling my hair gently as he reached in for a kiss, tasting the night before on his lips.

"I'll message you," he said, as I gathered my things and left the room.

"He called you an Uber, right?" Ads asked the next morning, calling me early to hear the goss.

"Nope, I called my Uber," I said. I could hear Ads groan and yell at

Dan, telling him he needed to sort Kiro out.

"I know you needed it, but he's not boyfriend material. I'm telling you early, do not get attached to him," she said. A part of me thought maybe I was different, that maybe I would be different. *Surely you can't share that kind of chemistry with everyone, right?* I never heard from him again and it felt empty. I even reached out and asked if he wanted to do something on one of the days before I left to go back to Hawaii, and he said he was too busy. It was good to tick it off the bucket list, but I knew this lifestyle wasn't for me. *Wonder if he will think of me again?*

15

Goals

After the excitement of the surprise wedding, it was all anyone could talk about. I realized I was quickly yesterday's news and the questions died down as quickly as they came which I was glad about. For the most part, people I weren't that close to forgot about me. It made me feel settled again. I felt comfortable meeting with friends, and found myself talking about events between Mark and me more comfortably. I spent time with my family and Adeline, who tried to get my mind off of Kiro, completely crashing their post-wedding vibe. The week flew by.

I knew before it was time to fly back to Hawaii I needed to move back to New York. I missed my friends and family. I missed the energy of the city. I also felt ready for a relationship again. I wanted to get clear on the kind of man I needed. It was time I started implementing Dr Lin's recommendations. Goals and affirmations. I wrote down the areas I wanted to focus on:

- RELATIONSHIP
- FINANCE
- LIFESTYLE

I stared at the words, not knowing what to write. *What do I want? What kind of life do I want to live?* It came to me that I didn't know what

I wanted. Leaving Mark only told me what I didn't want. I thought of Adeline's wedding, and how they described each other in their speeches.

I already wrote down the traits of my dream guy, but *how did I want my relationship to look?*

- FUN, DEEP CONVERSATIONS, JOINT CURIOSITY, MUTUAL EFFORT, CHEMISTRY, LOVE AND LAUGHTER

Then I wrote how I wanted my financial situation to look.

- I WANT TO MAKE $200,000 A YEAR WORKING TWENTY HOURS A WEEK
- THIS WILL BE THROUGH PHOTOGRAPHY SESSIONS, WHICH WILL MEAN AT LEAST FOUR SESSIONS PER WEEK
- THIS WILL MAKE EACH SESSION APPROXIMATELY $1,000 FOR MY TIME

This seemed achievable, although would require a rate increase.

What kind of lifestyle did I want? What did success look like to me?

- THREE OVERSEAS TRIPS PER YEAR
- NO ALARM CLOCK
- SELL MY PRINTS ONLINE
- WORK TWENTY HOURS PER WEEK, WHICHEVER DAYS REQUIRED

I could visually see my ideal lifestyle; how I wanted it to look and how I wanted it to feel. I worked out a budget based on my current income and current workload and included what my current expenses were.

Where do I want to live?

I thought again for a moment. *Where did I want to live?* I thought about Mom getting older, my siblings and Adeline being married now. I thought about Sel who would be in Oahu, and how beautiful and slow paced it was living near the beach. I thought about where I would want to raise my kids when the right person did finally come along. I wanted to be around my family. I wanted to be there for Ads. But I also knew I wanted to make more friends in Manhattan. When I lived with Mark, my world was small. Since travelling and living in Hawaii, my world had gotten so much bigger and I wanted it to continue that way, but I wanted to do it in Manhattan.

Then I began my affirmations, sitting there for longer than anticipated.

- I am healthy, happy and whole.
- I have a thriving photography business in Manhattan.
- I am in a kind and loving relationship.
- I have beautiful relationships with my family and friends.
- I am financially secure.
- I work twenty hours per week to earn $200k a year.
- I love travelling three times a year.

I wrote the same affirmations three times each. Each time, imagining all of them happening and how it felt to be there. I could see it and I could feel it. It was my phone that interrupted me.

"Want to head over for dinner?" Sel asked me over the phone.

"Can you head here, I'm just in the middle of something," I said, texting John soon after, that Sel was heading over and bringing us dinner. And within twenty minutes, she was there. A bottle of cabernet sauvignon and three poke bowls the hostel had as leftovers and were going to throw out at the end of the night.

"What's going on?" John asked at the table. He had been sitting in the lounge room watching the news but was the first to be up to open the door for Sel.

"I've officially decided guys, I'm moving back to Manhattan." I said, as Sel organized the wine glasses. "I'll work until whenever you need me John, but it's time. I'm thirty-five now and I do want to meet someone and have children, and I need to start working towards that. I'll fly back for photo shoots I already have booked or if I get them here. This is definitely my second home, and would love it if I could stay with one of you when I'm here. And John, you know Sel would make a great addition to your team if you're open to her taking over."

"Oh, I wouldn't expec ..." Sel started, surprised that I threw it out there.

"I was actually going to ask you, Sel. I do have a spare room now, and if you did want the role when Katie leaves, you're more than welcome to it." My heart fluttered. My favorite people helping each other. A reminder of how connections work, but also the beauty of things just falling into place.

"That would be great, John. I am share-housing now, but they are all super young and into parties. It would do me good to cut back the hours at the hostel and focus on work where I can actually use my skills. I used to work in finance in Portugal and will be able to support you with all of that too," she added. John nodded and held up his glass in cheers. I know he was disappointed about my decision to move back to New York, even though he knew it was coming.

"I'll miss you, you know," Sel said quietly.

"I know, Sel. I'll miss you too. You can come to Manhattan and stay with me any time, once I've got everything in order. I'm sure Mom will let me stay in the family home, but I will let you know. I have a few shoots here that I'll need to be back for, so it's definitely not the last you'll see of me," I said, "unless you want to come with me?" I joked.

"If I didn't love it so much here, Katie, I would. I need the ocean, and I love meeting so many travellers. This is where I need to be." I admired her, for knowing, and doing what she felt was right for her.

"Do you want to meet someone and have children?" I asked her. I was asking her the same questions I hated being asked, but I felt the question was coming from a different space. From a space of wanting to know her more, rather than for gossip.

"I would like to meet someone at some point. I don't think I want children. I want to continue going on adventures and travelling the world for the rest of my life. If I meet someone, great. If I don't, I'm happy experiencing the world as it is now." There was such an art to that, to being happy with the present, without putting any expectation on the future.

"What about you, John?" I asked, Sel curiously looking at him as well.

"I don't know, I don't think I'll ever meet someone open to my kind of lifestyle, but let's see. Who knows what will happen," he said cheerily, in true John form.

The night grew later, as we opened another bottle of wine and shared stories of our adventures, our hopes and dreams. We knew our time together was ticking. Goodbyes don't get any easier.

16

Mystery

I began working longer hours in the art gallery to get everything in order before I left. I put together processes and a guidebook for Sel, so she didn't walk in empty handed and have to figure it all out for herself, like I did. I put my images online, so I had access to it all and organized my own permissions on the system.

"Hello, welcome to Oresby Art Gallery, let me know how I can assist you," I said with a lullaby like tone, a softness to my voice knowing the times I greet strangers like this is slowly coming to an end. I watched from afar as a short European man nodded his head politely in response but didn't say anything. He walked to the first piece of artwork to his left, his eyes skimming over everything he was slowly passing. He was with a blonde woman, slim build and a sweet dimple on her right cheek. Her hair had a side part and the ends curled from the humidity, her eyes wide and excited. She was holding onto his arm, both dressed casually, like tourists.

"Anything I can help you with?" I asked. They shook their heads and kept wandering throughout the gallery. I always had the same curiosity with each person that came in. *Were they looking for something in particular? Were they actual buyers? Were they just browsing?* I continued to watch them as they stopped at one of the displays and stared. I saw her whisper something in his ear and he nodded, a warmth enveloping his face.

"Beautiful, isn't it?" I called out as I made my way slowly toward them. They nodded, wandered around more and then left. It wasn't unusual to have encounters like that on quiet days. I noticed the less people in the gallery usually the faster people walked through. I stood where they stopped, wondering what she had whispered to him. As I looked around, I started feeling heat in my face. I realized they had stopped at my wall. My wall. With all the pictures from my travels through Iceland, England, Scotland and Hawaii. The wall John had promised me if I looked after his gallery while he travelled. Staring fondly at the images before me, my heart fluttered, like it always did when I stood there reminiscing. My face always flushed when I was there. Not because people did or didn't ask about my work, but because it always felt like those travels were a dream, until I looked at those images, which reminded me it was real. I felt layers of gratitude every time I caught glimpses of them.

Quella's big smile beneath the Northern Lights. Gary's silhouette on the car that blissful evening before the Caleidh. I had a full wall of images, but those two were my favorite. Those moments and those people were etched into the core of me. *What were they doing right now? Would I ever get to see them again?* I had thought about calling them multiple times but would always remember at the most impractical moments, in the shower or driving. Then, the thought left me until another inconvenient moment.

Soon after the couple left, I received a strange call.

"Oresby Art Gallery, Katelyn speaking," I said, even though it was past five pm now and the shop was technically closed.

"Hi, I'd like to purchase one of the prints you have on the wall," said a man with a deep rustic voice; a voice that came straight from deep in the chest. His words took me by surprise. It was unusual someone calling to purchase. Usually they were walk-in buys or directly off the website without asking any questions. *Was that the guy who just came into the gallery?* The voice didn't seem to match if it was.

"Sure, which one?" I asked as I swivelled on the desk chair, bringing up the pieces on our online store. "And would you like to pay with credit card over the phone or would you like to go to our online store and make the purchase directly?"

"If I can just place it on hold, I will be in next week to pick it up," he said. A less unusual request.

"No problem, which piece was it?"

"Urmmm, it's the one with the code KATE987," he responded slowly, as if reading it from somewhere. I knew what print that was. It gave me butterflies thinking about it. The same reaction I felt every time I sold a copy of it.

"Oh yes, nice. I must admit, that's definitely one of my favorites!"

"Really," the caller began, "why is that, love?"

"Well … it looked like the world stood still for that moment, the way the light bounces off him. It feels calm and warm," I responded, my mind going back to that day when Gary was lying on the car, feeling the setting sun on my skin again.

"Sounds like I picked the right one then," he said with a cheeky chuckle. A familiar chuckle, but one I hadn't heard before.

"What name should I leave it under?"

"Mr O'Connor, please," he responded.

"Oh, are you from Scotland?"

"Ai," he said, as I finally noticed the familiar Scottish accent.

"This picture was actually taken just north of Edinburgh, although I couldn't tell you where exactly, but I loved the place."

"You don't say. That's probably why I liked it. Anyway, love, I have to go now. I will see you this time next week at, say, eleven am?"

"We open at ten am, I'll be here from then, Mr O'Connor," I finally said, as we both hung up the phone, a smile easing my face and warmth cascading throughout my body.

As I started getting the piece prepared to store away, I blushed slightly as I thought of Gary. I still hadn't even shown him this picture and here I was selling it to strangers. *Was I even allowed to? Maybe it was time to tell him?* I only got as far as adding him on social media a few months ago. It took him months to accept me because he's never on it. He never posted, and I didn't know if it was weird that I requested him as a *friend.* Alice never mentioned him when we spoke, neither did Uncle Pat, so it felt like one of those people who were just around for a season. And I could appreciate that for what it was.

I walked to my apartment that evening with a little bounce in my step, wondering who Mr O'Connor was and how he found the picture. It made me want to tell someone, anyone. It made me want to tell Alice. I had been meaning to call her anyway so maybe this was a sign to finally do it.

Ring-ring-ring-ring-ring.

"Kate, you don't know what time it is here do you?" she answered, with a croaky voice.

"Ali, someone just bought that print of Gary from when I was in Edinburgh, and it made me think of you," I said.

"Oh, that's nice," she responded, with no enthusiasm in her voice.

"What time is it there, it can't be that late?" I asked her, trying to make it seem like it wasn't a big deal no matter what the time was.

"Eleven hours, Katie, it's four-thirty am here."

"Oh, bugger, okay, well, thanks for picking up. Call me soon? I also wanted to tell you that I'm moving back to Manhattan in the next couple months as well."

"Really? Manhattan? I'll call you back later. Love you," she responded just before hanging up, not even answering my question. I still felt like celebrating though, so I headed over to the hostel to see who was working. *Maybe someone would be up for a drink?*

"KATE!" Sel excitedly yelled when she saw me walking up the stairs.

"Oh, thank God you're working. What time do you finish? Want to go for a drink after?" I asked her, crossing my fingers she wasn't working all night.

"Sorry, babe, I'm on the graveyard shift," she said, "but come around this side and let's open a bottle, we don't have too many booked check-ins."

"Suits me!" I said as I opened the reception door to join her. There was a small bar fridge under the desk where they left beers and snacks for whoever had the long night shift. There were also a few bottles of wine hidden from when they confiscated them from the travellers who didn't abide by the open alcohol policy in the dorm rooms. I opened a bottle and poured us both glasses of wine while sitting on the cushions on the floor next to her, almost hidden, so people couldn't see us.

"What's going on?" she asked me, smiling as she took her first sip. She knew something was up.

"Well, someone bought one of my images today," I told her, closing my eyes as I gave her a cheesy grin, "the Gary one."

"Not the Gary one," she smirked. She knew how much it meant to me. "Who was it?" She didn't know every detail about Gary, but she asked about the photo when she saw it at the art gallery one day and could tell there was something there, just by the way I told her about him.

"I don't know. It wasn't a walk-in. Someone called and placed the order, so they may have seen it online or been told about it," I told her shrugging, taking another sip. "But he will be in next week to pick it up so I'll ask him about it!" She congratulated me, leaning over to give me a big embrace. While she was hugging me, I added, "God, it's going to suck to leave you."

"I know." And after a silent moment, "Want to go on a quick trip together?" she asked. My face instantly and instinctively lit up. I had been so busy working on the business and looking after John's shop and exploring Hawaii over the last year, I forgot about the rest of the world.

The whole reason I ended up here in the first place is because I wanted to travel more.

"Well, these backpackers came in the other day and they were talking about these ayurvedic retreats in India. They showed me videos and had amazing things to say about it. I would love to go now that I have work at John's gallery coming up. It's the perfect time for you before you start your life again in Manhattan too. And let's be real, John owes you one." We sat in the corner of the reception area, tucked away, sipping on our wine as she flicked through photos, on her phone, of the retreat she was talking about.

"India? John has been raving about it too. I haven't asked him many questions about it because I didn't want to sound naive, but isn't it like, really busy with lots of people and ... like ... dirty?" I asked naively, embarrassed as I was saying it, knowing that New York had leaking plumbing pipes mixed with restaurant wastewater that drip out onto the street and sidewalks.

"That's what I asked them, but they recommended Kerala in the south or Goa, which I learned was colonized by the Portuguese, so it would actually be super interesting to go?" I thought for a moment but realized she was right. I didn't want to go from building a life in Hawaii to building a life in Manhattan without doing something for me. I had enough money and John did owe me.

"Let's do it," I said, getting goosebumps over my entire body, a feeling I've grown to call 'truth bumps'. That's how I knew it was the right move.

"Confirm with John and then we'll meet up to figure out flights and dates?" she said, her eyes glistening with excitement in the light. We clinked our plastic cups, and I made a mental note to chat with John and get his recommendations from his trip. *India? Were we really going to India?*

17

Surprise

"Next you're going to ask me if you can buy my art gallery, aren't you?" John joked in response to asking him about India. "I think it's a brilliant idea, you'll love it. It's nothing like I've seen before," he said, as I was about to walk out the door. "Selina better not get used to it though, I'm not letting her galivant around the world like I did because she's your friend you know?" he added. This time I didn't know if he was joking. It seemed drier, but surely, he was.

"Trust me, she will be the second-best employee you'll ever have. Keep her happy," I said cheekily walking out the door on my way to the art gallery.

I wasn't at the art gallery for long before the chime went off and I heard a few people walk in. In all the excitement about going to India, I had completely forgotten about Mr O'Connor coming in at eleven am. When I saw who it was, I instantly burst into tears. I couldn't believe who was standing in front of me. No words could come out of my mouth as I stood there, my head buried in my hands. They slowly walked to me, awkwardly, unsure with my response.

"Are these happy tears, love?" Uncle Pat asked, as Alice ran up to me, wrapping me up with her arms. I stood there and nodded, but my head was still buried. The emotions were so overwhelming.

"I'm happy to see you too," Alice said, giggling and whispering in my ear. I took a deep breath and went to hug Uncle Pat. Then, I saw him, standing there, embarrassed almost.

"Gary?" He winked at me as he walked up to hug me. I felt tingles throughout my entire body, "Wait. Mr O'Connor?"

"It was my brother who called up. That print is mine and I still want it though," he said, the cheek spreading across his face, knowing they had gotten such a surprise out of me.

"But why? How? I still don't understand?" I asked them all in disbelief. *Why was everyone coming to Hawaii and not telling me first so I could emotionally prepare?*

"Well, love. It came to our attention that we were all in need of a holiday and Alice said that you were moving back to Manhattan. We wanted to take the opportunity to see you while you were still here in Hawaii." Uncle Pat said to me with humor in his voice. He held my chin softly and wiped away a tear with his thumb, my heart heating.

"Where are you staying? How did you find me? I have so many questions!"

"What time do you knock off?" Alice asked me, not answering any of them.

"Honestly, I just got here but let me call John and I know he will come in and take over for the rest of the day." I ran back behind the desk to get my phone and called John.

"My family has surprised me from Scotland, do you mind coming in?" I asked him.

"Another favor, this is getting ridiculous?" he chuckled, "I'll be there in ten. Just put the sign up and you can head off," he said.

"Wait for me outside while I lock up and then we can head to the bar around the corner?," I asked, as I watched them file outside one by one, adrenaline rushing through my body, my mind swirling with excitement.

It was the dose of love I was needing at precisely the right time. As I closed the gallery door, I remembered to run back in and get the print I had neatly packaged already for 'Mr O'Connor' – the silhouette of him on top of his car, as the sun was setting, before going to his mom's house for dinner. Not once thinking this could have been the reason for yesterday's odd purchase. *Did Alice tell him about it? And why was 'he' here?*

18

Family

I led them to The Hideout, and we sat in the open alfresco area where we could talk but also people-watch. We could hear the laughter and chatter from the beach, and if we looked out a little further into the distance, we could see people playing volleyball. They would be there until the sun set and only dark figures could be made out. The bartenders knew my name because of how often Sel and I were there we pulled up chairs and I gestured for them to bring us four mai tais.

"So, what's been happening?" I asked, looking at them all, still bewildered they were sitting in front of me.

"You're asking us, are you?" Alice responded cheekily, raising an eyebrow.

"Oh, leave the lass alone," Uncle Pat piped in.

Gary was the only one who didn't make a comment; he seemed to not know what to say. I didn't either. I knew they were asking me about Mark, but I didn't know where to start.

"You're right. It's been a year," I began. "Alice knows a bit and I don't know how much she shared with you, but long story short, we ended up getting into a massive argument after a few days of being here and I couldn't take it anymore. I think we knew how different we were and tried our best. After an argument one night, over him asking my ex-boss for my job back without asking me first, I woke up and he'd left. He bought my share of the house off me which essentially has been supporting the last year and I've just been living here. In summary."

"I honestly can't believe the numpty left you like that," Uncle Pat started, but Alice touched his arm in an effort to allow me to continue. I could see the fury rise in Gary as well.

"I didn't know what to do to be honest with you. I wasn't ready to go back to Manhattan, or back to Edinburgh. I was confused and John gave me somewhere to live and work," I continued on, this time Gary looking at me curiously. "I met him at the hotel, and he owns the gallery you came into, he literally saw me the morning after Mark left. We went on a hike and we just got along so well."

"Why didn't you call us when it all happened?" Alice asked, clearly upset with me. It wasn't just her. It took me a few months to tell anyone outside of Ads.

"I needed my own time, my own space." I held my hand out onto the table so I could hold hers. "I was embarrassed and felt a bit of shame around it, trying to process everything by myself."

"How are you? Now, I mean?" Gary asked, looking just as concerned as Alice and Uncle Pat.

"I'm doing well now, thank you. My photography business has done really well here. I went back to New York for my friend's wedding last month and decided it was time for me to move home, to see my Luna again and just be around my friends, family and Mom. Mom and Derrick are getting old too," I said. Alice nodded, agreeing. I knew that's why she stayed in Edinburgh too, for Uncle Pat.

"Enough about me. I want to hear what's been going on with you guys," I said.

Uncle Pat began telling me all the gossip about relatives I had met while I was there, Alice talked about work and was glad she was able to take leave, and Gary for the most part just sat there letting us have our moment together.

"And what about you, Gary? What made you want to join these two?" I finally said, curious.

"It was his idea," Uncle Pat chimed in, nodding his head while raising his eyebrows, somewhat proud giving Gary the credit he knew he deserved.

"Alice came into the pub last week, the day she spoke to you, and said you were moving back. They had talked about visiting you for the last year, so I said, why not now. I kind of thought the idea out and that they should surprise you. Next thing you know, we were a few pints deep, the pub had shut and we were sitting around the table buying tickets and booking accommodation." They all laughed in agreeance. I didn't say anything, I didn't know what to say. I didn't even think they were thinking about me. I had convinced myself that no-one really cared what I was doing, or that I didn't need to burden them.

"Well, I'm glad those beers brought you here." I took a sip of my mai tai and continued, "Oh, Gary. While you're here. Do I have your consent to sell pictures of you?"

Gary laughed as I handed him his print.

"You're really good at this, Katie," he said, admiring the photo. He passed the print to Alice, who then passed it onto Uncle Pat, their eyes gleaming with pride.

The evening turned into night, the cocktails turned into wine and whisky, and story after story was filled with laughter. The cup I didn't even know needed filling was being filled.

19

Tourist

The timing of Uncle Pat, Alice and Gary was perfect. They didn't realize the next day was Monday, and on Mondays, the gallery was closed. It meant I could play tour guide for them. I'd only had Ads visit me and was excited to show them around.

"You didn't!" I said as Alice let me into their two-bedroom apartment that overlooked Waikiki Beach. Uncle Pat's famous French toast wafting through the apartment as I walked in. The apartment had a cosy, beach feel to it, with a wooden-cross-Hampton style.

The table was set on the balcony with orange juice and coffee, the backdrop of the sparkling and vast ocean set the mesmerizing scene. Uncle Pat put the French toast in the middle of the table and gestured for everyone to sit down.

"Where's Gary?" I asked as I sat, the warm ocean breeze blowing through my hair.

"Miss me already, eh?" he said as he walked through the sliding timber doors onto the balcony, his cheeky grin reminding me of the first moment we met, when he kissed my hand and wrote his number on it. I didn't say anything, I didn't need to as the corner of my lips angled up and my cheeks slightly blushing, said it all. "I'm staying next door to them. I haven't bunked with anyone in a long while, I thought it would be better for our relationship."

"I called your mom after you left Edinburgh," Uncle Pat said, out of nowhere, interrupting Gary, who winked at me when he said he had the room next door.

"You what?" I responded, surprised no-one had told me before that moment. "She never told me and I've spoken to her many times."

"I asked her not to. You had so much going on and it was better to talk to you about it face to face," he said. I wasn't ready to admit that was true.

"What did you say? What did she say? What did you talk about?"

"Nothing much. We just caught up over the last few years and I told her we looked after you and thanked her for giving you our details," he said nonchalantly. "It really meant so much that you came to visit, Katie."

"I feel the same, Uncle Pat. I was just thinking how lovely it would have been if she was here with the rest of the family. Mom, Derrick, Teanna and Jarrod … it would have been so nice if you could all meet again in person."

"One day," Uncle Pat said, "I know it will happen one day." I knew it was true as well. I knew one day everyone would be together … maybe if I ever got married or had children.

"There is a surfing competition on at the Pipeline, I think we should check that out first," I told them, knowing they would be in awe with how big the waves were and the sheer strength of the surfers making their way out to sea. We finished breakfast, cleaned up and then I drove, first stopping at the pineapple plantation on the way to get some ice cream. When we got there, we found a spot beneath the shade of a palm tree and watched on.

"To be honest, I didn't think I would enjoy this," Alice said, her eyes locked onto a huge wave as it crushed one of the surfers that disappeared under the water momentarily,

"I didn't I think I would either. They paddle for so long to get … nowhere." I pointed to one of the surfers who had just gotten into the water. We watched him as his arms pushed and pushed against the current, the wind moving him sideways and barely making any tracks. It took him about twenty minutes to get to where he needed to be, finding a space between the surfers and body boarders. All that effort without knowing they would even catch a wave.

"Those waves are ridiculous, is it like fifty feet?" Uncle Pat asked Gary, who shrugged and continued looking on with awe. The beach was busy, sirens were being tooted, children were screaming with glee and exhilaration and I'm pretty sure we were all getting sunburned, so after a couple of hours of chasing the shadows of the tree, I was ready to leave, and they had no choice but to come with me.

"Anyone for ahi tacos?" I asked, my stomach started growling as I looked at the time. No-one said anything, but everyone stood up. We went to my favorite taco food truck and then continued to drive around the island that day, stopping at different beaches or blow holes and making sure we were back in the apartment for the sunset, so we could pour our drinks and relax in each other's company again. It was my favorite part of the day.

A surreal warmth enveloped me as I sat with them again, a mixture of nuts and chips on the table, while Alice and I moved onto white wine and the men continued with beer. I was watching the shadows on their faces change as the sun moved closer to the ocean, not wanting to forget any part of this moment with them. It felt surreal to have them here, and I was so grateful.

20

Moments

The next day, I headed back to work while Uncle Pat, Alice and Gary continued their sight-seeing with the intention to meet up with them at the end of the day for dinner. I had written a list of all the things they could do, and it seemed they would be doing their own things, with one going to Pearl Harbor and another snorkelling at Hanauma Bay.

"What are you doing?" he said with a deep, thick, Scottish accent. I knew who it was. He came to visit me at the gallery.

"I thought you were going snorkelling today?" I said to him.

"I actually wanted to hike up Diamond Head, but Uncle Pat and Alice weren't interested, so I did it myself and then went for a swim … and then decided to come and see you." I instantly felt nervous. The last time we had spent time together alone was when I took that photo of him on his car, it took me back to that moment, lying there next to him. "I wanted to see you alone so I can make sure you're comfortable with me being here, if you're not, I can go home, no hard feelings or anything," he added. *Did he mean that?*

"No, not at all. I appreciate you coming here so much," I said. "And how beautiful is the view from the top of Diamond Head? That's actually where John took me the day after Mark and I broke up, and the reason

I'm here today."

"It was gorgeous. It's a beautiful place, I was surprised to hear you were moving back to Manhattan," he said, somehow it suddenly felt serious, heat rushed to my face. "I also hoped you would call me at some point, but I didn't want to intrude. You would have been going through so much, but I regret not checking in on you. Alice didn't say much to me to start with," he continued on.

"I was going to call you about the image, but it never felt like the right time," I responded. "To be honest, I think the last year I have just been hiding away and not dealing with a lot of what happened. I have thought about you though. What have you been up to? You haven't said much, but I know it's because you are giving the rest of us time to catch up."

"Just spending time with the family, Mum is getting older. The bar is doing great though. I've actually received a job opportunity to be a joint owner of a restaurant opening in New York," he said, his eyes making direct contact with mine. I felt a rush around my body, a tingle, trying to figure out if he was subconsciously trying to tell me something. "Then when I heard you were moving back, it made me want to talk to you about it."

"That's amazing, congratulations. What are you going to do?" I asked, wondering if he was going to take the opportunity.

"I don't know. What do you think? Do you think I would like Manhattan? I like the slow life but you've really inspired me to move out of my comfort zone, Katie, you truly have." I could feel myself blushing. Inspirational was the last thing I thought about my situation.

"I think if that's your first instinct, you should definitely do it, what have you got to lose?" I said, "And I'm moving to Manhattan because I miss my family. I've been able to experience moving away, which is great, but it's not for me, and it's taken me a while to realize it's okay to change your mind," I said, feeling it honestly to my core.

"I think you're right," he said. "Where will you be living in Manhattan? Might need to hit you up when I get there. You would be the only person I know."

"You'll make a tonne of friends. Mom is letting me stay in the house I grew up in. Honestly, if you wanted to stay a while until you get everything sorted, you're more than welcome," I added, not knowing whether I'd need to check with my mother first. I had an urge to be close to him. Partly feeling closer to him because he wanted my advice, and the other part knowing we always had this connection, like we've known each other in another lifetime. I know we both felt it. I walked up and kissed him.

"Oh wow, I'm so sorry," I said, immediately pulling myself back. He pulled me back in closer and kissed me again. Silence followed. *Can someone just say something already?*

"You know how I've felt about you since the day I saw you. I know we both have felt it," he said, finally filling the silence, his voice soft, almost a whisper, as I felt his hands caressing the side of my neck. It was true. We both knew it.

"I didn't expect to do that," I started saying, but I didn't know what words to use that would explain how I felt or why I kissed him, so I paused and instead pulled him even closer once more and kissed him again. It was a perfect moment, his body pressed against mine. I could hear the ocean crashing in the background and smell his cologne. *Was this a good idea?*

21

Finally

Gary, Alice and Uncle Pat stayed the entire week. They met Sel and John, and we enjoyed eating and drinking our way through different restaurants and bars. Gary and I would sneak kisses and touches when no-one was looking, enjoying the growing comfort between us. We didn't talk about Manhattan again and I didn't look at my piece of paper from Dr Lin to make sure I was doing the right thing. I wanted to enjoy our connection while it was there, for whatever it was and for however long it may be. It didn't feel like a one-night stand, like with Kiro, it felt much more than that. It always had.

I wondered if Gary expected something to happen between us and that was why he stayed in the apartment next door to Uncle Pat and Alice. The first few nights, after that kiss, we would stagger our goodbyes and go back to his room, open a bottle of wine and talk late into the night.

The first night we had sex was unexpected, we staggered our goodbyes with everyone as usual and met at the beach. We walked for miles as the moonlight glistened against the ocean water, the waves crashing against our feet, as Gary held our shoes in one hand and relaxed the other around my waist, the night breeze gently pushing our bodies closer together.

There was something innately different about this night, like there were more magical moments between us than an exchange of words.

"How have you had enough of this?" Gary asked as we found an isolated area on the sand to sit, looking out into the darkness, the source of the sounds and salty scents.

"I haven't, but it will always be here to visit. I miss my family and friends too much" I said, resting my head on his shoulder. I held his arm with both of mine, entwined. His bicep innocently flexed as he wrapped his arm around my neck, causing my body to naturally melt into his, my lips softening on his for a kiss. The weight of my body slowly pushing into his until we both were laying in the sand. I moved one leg around his body to straddle him, the cold sand pressing into my knees. I began grinding my waist back and forth, feeling his dense jeans through one thin layer of fabric as my dress naturally moved up. I closed my eyes to embrace all the sensations as Gary's beard rubbed against my face and his hands massaged the side of my thighs, tighter and tighter until he was gripping my cheeks firmly, supporting my movements.

"Here? Are you sure?" he said, our gaze meeting finally. I bit my lip and nodded as I felt myself moisten. Our eyes were locked as his strength rolled me onto my back. He delicately kissed me and then began moving down my body, first kissing between my chest, then the fabric above my belly – taking off my underwear as he was doing it. His head disappeared between my legs as I relaxed my neck backwards. He moaned in pleasure at what he was tasting, the vibration making me tingle even more. I closed my eyes, marvelling that I didn't need to give him any direction, like he had been here before, the way he inserted both fingers rhythmically   the right pace, the right depth, the right time. I curled my tailbone inward as he felt the movement of my body and added matched pressure with the same pace.

"Faster," I gasped in a soft breath. He listened, slowly increasing the flick of his fingers inside me as my body squirmed beneath him, a groan of pleasure in his voice once more, as I came into his mouth, electricity running throughout my entire body. I pulled his shirt toward me, wiping my moisture off his beard, kissing him while I unbuttoned and unzipped his pants. The kiss wasn't delicate this time, his tongue going deep into my mouth, passionately. I could see his eyes were on a mission when we both took a breath. I watched him take my body in. "I want you inside me," I whispered. He pulled himself out of his pants but didn't insert it fully, teasing me until I held it in my hand myself, his thickness pulsing largely into my hand to the same beat of my body. I rubbed it against me, our eyes locked, then angled my hips up while he thrust slowly inside me. We both moaned in relief, like the year of built-up tension between us had finally released.

"Wow," Gary said, as we lay on the cold sand, catching our breath after a few more intense minutes.

"I know," I responded, looking up at the stars, feeling my chest rise and fall intensely. "It's exactly as I imagined it to be," I admitted out loud. I saw him nodding in the corner of my eye, a look of satisfaction on his face. My mind naturally wandered to being here a year ago, crying on the beach alone. *Who thought I would be here? Finally, so happy and so grateful?*

He pulled my body closer to his like he knew he needed to, grains of sand scattered between us, "It's exactly how it's meant to be, Katie."

22

Caught

"I'm not complaining but I'm looking forward to having you back when they all leave. I've missed you," said John one night at dinner, a quick seemingly unintentional snort coming from Sel. Gary and I looked at each other, Uncle Pat and Alice looked at each other too.

"Oh, you mean the late nights," I chuckled, hoping no one would realize I hadn't been going home at all and that I'd been living from a bag of clothes in Gary's room. John looked confused, and when he quickly realized what was happening, he smirked, which was so far from subtle it made everyone catch on. Everyone seemed to smile. I cringed, feeling like a high school teenager who'd been caught sneaking around after school by her parents. It was family after all.

"Yes, sure, the late nights," he chuckled, taking a sip of his beer and looking directly at me.

"Guys, you know we all know right? Can we just talk about it?" Alice piped up, confidence oozing from the three empty mai tais sitting in front of her.

"Know what?" I pretended to sound confused.

"I think everyone's caught on, babe," Sel chimed in, a light-hearted chuckle escaping her.

"They know," Gary interjected, his words tinged with amusement, clearly not wanting to play this game any longer. His teeth shining brightly, the corners of his eyes slanting upward with the slight wrinkles that formed from years of laughter. Urgh.

"Do they know about New York too?" I gave up easily. *Who were we kidding?* The sneaking was fun for a little while, but now they were leaving, it was also probably time to talk about what his next moves were and we hadn't had a chance. Gary nodded.

"You all knew?" I said, my tone reflecting my baffled excitement. A range of emotions tightly knotted inside of me, finally beginning to unravel outside of me.

"Well, we didn't know what would happen with Gary and New York, but we did know it was one of the reasons Gary suggested the trip. We told him to join and see how things felt, and you were obviously the best person to ask questions to if he took the offer." A part of me was upset Alice hadn't told me, but I also knew it had nothing to do with her, and I couldn't be.

"Have you decided?" I asked Gary.

"I have." He turned to John to fill him in. "I've been offered a business partnership to open a restaurant in New York. I didn't know whether to take it and when Alice told me Katie was moving back, I thought I would ask some questions about life there as I'm not one for social media."

"And, by the look of it you got more than some questions answered," he said, cheering the air. Gary closed his eyes and shook his head, the smile not leaving his face.

"You should have heard how she spoke about you and that picture," Sel added, my face blushing.

"It had been a year, and I didn't want to put any pressure on Katie, just wanted to see how things went. But it looks like we feel the exact same way about each other still," he said, pleased.

Gary started talking about the restaurant, and how it had already done very well in Edinburgh, and how the owners of the restaurant came into the pub, met Gary and got along so well with him, which didn't surprise anyone except Gary. They came in two more nights in a row, and by this time, Gary already knew what they wanted to drink and would have it ready for their arrival. Not because of who they were, but because that was his style, that was the family feel and the culture he had created there. That's how he treated everyone and that's what they liked about him. That's what everyone loved about him.

"You don't see this kind of passion and care very often," one of them said to him. "Would you be interested in a bit of a sea change?" Gary declined them twice, but they kept on coming in, offering him more and more money, and then ultimately, a share of the business, while showing them the financials for the current restaurant in Edinburgh.

"I would be a fool not to take it and at least given it a try," he said, looking toward me and our eyes intensely meeting. *Was he talking about the business, or me?*

"Wait, so you already signed the contract?" I asked, curious. He nodded.

"I had to do it. I was always going to do it. And then when I heard you were moving back, I thought, Wow. What are the chances of everything lining up like this?"

"It's always worth the risk," John said. "This is what life's about, trying new things and seeing what happens." A playfulness to his voice, like always.

There was a moment of silence, with everyone soaking up the conversation. Not an awkward silence, but a reflective one. I began to think back to how I risked quitting my job, travelling solo and leaving Mark. I knew I needed to change course, and it was beautiful to see Gary receive an opportunity to change too. And now a trip to India with my new best friend I met a few months ago. There is something surreal and overwhelming about knowing we can craft the life we desire. Once a decision is made, everything finds its way of falling into place.

"Speaking of which, how is the India trip planning going?" John said, like he could read my mind. Everyone had their eyes on me now. I hadn't had a moment to tell them we were going. It was my turn to speak up.

"Sel and I are going to India for four weeks before I head back here and then to Manhattan," I told everyone. "But it's going well. We have booked it for two weeks time and are staying at a resort by the ocean in Goa. We'll be there for New Year's Eve. Then we are going to a jungle retreat in Kerala. Someone recommended the retreat to Sel at the hostel and it turned out it was the same place John had been when he was there before he came back to Oahu. It's a yoga and ayurvedic retreat."

"We don't yoga though," Sel quickly said.

"And we don't really ayurdvedic either," I laughed, quickly adding, "but am sure it will be a great experience."

"An adventure," she added this time. We exchanged glances, excitement dancing in our eyes, as goosebumps, or truth bumps, spread across my skin. "The backwaters are so beautiful. If you have a chance, go to Munnar where the spice and tea plantations are. The winding roads and mountains are incredible, it looks like something from a land before time," John chimed in. Uncle Pat had also been to India, and so the conversation continued about the food, the people, the culture. Alice, Sel and I listened and asked questions as they continued to discuss it. Gary though, was looking at me, smiling. I could feel his eyes as I tried to focus on the conversation even though I was ready for everyone to pack up and leave so we could spend some time together. *I wonder what the future will bring for us.*

23

Chaos

As soon as Gary, Alice and Uncle Pat left, Sel and I quickly changed focus to India.

"What do I pack for India?" I asked Sel over the phone. "Can we wear shorts and tank tops, will it be hot?"

"Yes, you can," John yelled from the lounge room, overhearing our conversation. "Tourists wear all the short stuff there, but it depends if you will feel comfortable with people staring. Modesty will always be your best bet though." I googled different packing lists and read blogs on what people took: tropical insect repellent, diarrhoea medication and pain killers. I knew I had to take my camera. I still adored the one Mom and Derrick gave me before I left on my trip last year.

"Do we need all these vaccinations too?" I asked, looking at another list I googled.

"We don't need all that, I'm sure of it," Sel would say, me learning quickly she's a very chill traveller. I, on the other hand, needed lists and confirmation. I was going to be prepared for whatever came at me. We had planned on going to Goa first, so we could party, eat and drink and then detox and relax for two weeks at the retreat in the jungle. We didn't really know what we were setting ourselves up for, but we figured that was the beauty of it. I don't think I would have done India alone, but there was a comfort with Sel, with how confident and adventurous she was.

John was looking after the art gallery, and I had booked the Uber for the afternoon. *Why had I left packing to the day of the flight?* I felt I was still a bit of an amateur with long-distance travelling, and I was a bit rusty given it had been a while since my last holiday. The flight was over thirty hours to Goa, the cheapest one stopping in Seattle and Doha before getting to our destination. We organized our hotel to pick us up from the airport because we didn't know if we could Uber or what to expect, it was one less thing we needed to worry about. I'm glad we did.

"This looks like chaos," I said to Sel as we walked out of the arrival gate, an ick in my stomach from exhaustion and craving a shower. We had followed the crowd through customs, making the wrong turn a few times and having to turn back because we didn't know where to get the immigration documents from. They turned out to be on a table with no signage. The first thing I noticed, once we got through immigration, were the men. There were men standing everywhere, coming up to us asking if we needed help or transport. Sel had a new confidence I'd never seen before. I watched as she walked ahead of me, her eyes scanning all the men to see our names. She waved at someone, as I realized he was holding up a sign with our names on it.

"How did you see that?" I asked her. The writing on the signage was small and hard to decipher between all the other signs. Sel looked at me, a cheeky grin forming that favorite dimple of mine, and winked. I felt so safe with her.

"Katelyn and Selina?" a slim Indian man said. He had short black hair with a beard and looked about mid-forties. He had a bit of charm to him, a smile that created instant ease within me.

"Yes, that's us," I said, as he grabbed both of our bags and politely asked us to follow him. As we walked out of the airport, the warm breeze enveloped me. It was intriguing to be in a country where most people had brown skin. The diversity was both captivating and eye-opening. I know it was naive to think, already coming from a place like New York, which has so many diverse cultures, but this was something else – I found myself fascinated by my new surroundings and caught myself staring – only to notice that I was often being stared back at. The driver told us to wait for a few moments while he grabbed the car, while we waited, we people-watched.

"John said we could wear singlets and shorts?" I said, looking around not seeing either. All the men were in polo or button-up shirts with long pants and sneakers, even though it felt about eighty-six degrees Fahrenheit. There were a few women, their long straight hair tied to the bottom of their scalp and all wearing the same style – long-sleeved blouses, jeans and ballet type flats or sandals.

"Maybe he meant at the beach?" she assured me, seeing the concern on my face.

The driver beeped at us from a few metres away to grab our attention, and then pulled up beside us, jumping back out to put our bags in the car while we got into the back seat.

"It will be about an hour to your hotel, please feel free to nap. If you need me to pull over to get anything, just let me know. There are two bottles of water in the back for you," he said in broken English. It was midday, we were both hungry but were happy to wait until we got to the hotel to check in and grab a drink and food. I wasn't sure about side street snacks yet.

I watched as we drove through the streets, the main word always coming to my mind being *chaos*. The multiple electric cables wildly running through the streets were looped together and tied near the street signs. There were people everywhere and no-one seemed to abide by any traffic rules, horns beeping every second. There were lines on the road, but everyone was driving on them, not between them. There seemed to be lights, but no-one was paying attention to them either, and there was also roundabouts where no-one was giving way. There were little balls of metal with three wheels that I later found out were called *tuk tuks*, that had a higher pitch horn then a car. And there were mopeds everywhere. Everyone was beeping, but from what I could see, it wasn't for an emergency, like the rules were at home, it was seemingly to let someone know they were near them or approaching. People were walking through the street, or across the street. at any point, almost dancing between the traffic like an art form. There were stray dogs, somehow all kinds of breeds, that also didn't seem concerned by the noise, the rubbish or the people. Chaos, but somehow organized chaos. It was strange to me that there were no crashes, maybe because everyone was driving at around twenty-four miles per hour … and interesting that crashes at home would happen with one-tenth of the traffic, but due to being at higher speeds. It was intense. My central nervous system was in shock. *How were we going to cope here for a month?*

24

Goa

We stayed at a resort in Anjuna for the first week of our Goa leg. Sel was told this is where the European vibe beach clubs were, with stunning ocean views, good food and more tourists which made wearing a bikini comfortable. Sel's connections were not wrong. The place was stunning.

The hotel was four stars and had a balcony overlooking the ocean on a cliff, palm trees perfectly positioned. We could walk down to the beach if we wanted to go for a swim in the ocean or have a drink by it, or we could stay in our bungalow-style room and swim in the infinity pool. It depended if we wanted people around, or not. I took my camera everywhere, wanting to capture it all so I would remember its distinct beauty.

Our hotel was attached to a restaurant-type night club. It looked to be an outdoor restaurant, but the first night we stayed, there was a DJ and everyone was dancing on the balcony. People were smoking too, which I was not used to with the smoking laws back home. I took photos of the smoke disappearing into the night sky. We entered the venue through what looked like a cave, and ascended up some narrow stairs and then descended into a spectacular view of the ocean stretching to meet the horizon framed by swaying palm trees.

"Where are you from?" a group of guys at a neighboring table asked on our second night, as we were watching the sunset with cocktails in hand. It was NYE, something I didn't tend to celebrate much but I knew Sel did. We came early, only being next door, and the crowds had just started rushing in. We watched as everyone walked from the entryway to the table, one fist-pumping the air to the beat of the music, the other one carrying a drink, many with a cigarette between their fingers.

"I'm from the US and Sel is Portuguese," I said, speaking for Sel to make things easier. They were quite attractive, wearing light button-up shirts, linen shorts and dress shoes. They had flown in from Mumbai for a friend's wedding and NYE, and were in Goa for two days. They introduced themselves as Rhyn, Lloyd, Payal and Pratik.

"Are you staying close by?" they asked.

"Just next door," I said, pointing at the rows of bungalows across from us.

"They are beautiful," one of the guys said. "Have you been anywhere else around here?" We both shook our heads.

"Just got in yesterday, we could hear the music from our room last night and the staff highly recommended it so thought we better check it out," Sel chuckled, "and am glad we did," she said, turning her heard toward the sunset, the glow of the sun's rays on her face made her sparkle.

"I recommend you go to the Mayan Beach Club, Olive and Calamari … all really great places," one of the guys in the group said. "Have you tried Goan food yet?" they continued on, which made us look at each other at the same time and instantly giggle.

"We tried the prawn curry last night, but it was too spicy," I said, scrunching my face up and covering my mouth with my hands like I was tasting the chilli all over again, needing a sip to cool my hallucinating mouth down.

"Aloo chops. Aloo is potato. Any fish curry. Try the vindaloo, but that will be very spicy. Chicken cafreal and the xacuti," he said, as I had my phone out spelling them the best I could.

"Desserts?" Sel asked.

"You will see bebinca on every menu. Maybe try the falooda." He was looking into the air, like he was looking for more ideas or inspiration. "Oh, and go to the Fontainhas area in Panaji, that's a pretty cool place I think you will like."

We continued talking about life in the States and how it was in India, him sharing how he travels an hour for work, and that his day starts at seven am and he doesn't get home until eight pm. A part of me didn't want to share the lifestyle I was living in Hawaii, it would have felt like a dream to them.

I really liked the people so far. While some women may have thought they were flirting unwantedly, they were just out with friends wanting to meet and chat to new people, there was nothing sleazy about it. They offered a round of drinks, but we didn't know the etiquette or the expectation and politely declined, saying it was lovely to meet them. They came back with two cocktails, told us to have a great night and joined their bigger group of friends.

"Think it's safe?" I asked Sel, once they handed them to us and walked away.

"Usually if they're going to do anything dodgy, they tend to hang around, right?" she said. She took a sip, shrugged her shoulders and kept drinking, knocking it back quickly. When nothing happened, I followed suit. Between food, drinks and dancing, we continued to talk to strangers, asking for recommendations on what to do and where to eat, adding it all to our list. We finished the night kissing strangers on the cheek during the countdown, Sel disappearing with her goodnight kiss and me calling Gary. The next day, hungover by the pool, we googled all the places we were recommended and saw how far they were from us; all within an hour's drive, which made it accessible.

We planned our next two days sight-seeing around Goa, marvelling at the views, the bright red sunsets and the warm salty ocean on our bodies. We didn't get used to the high numbers of men, or the fact they kept staring or trying to sell some ocean sport activity during our beach walks, but quickly learned they were harmless. We learned that tipping the guys serving us drinks on the beach would mean we would have our belongings looked after while we went swimming together, and they would always make recommendations on what to eat and what to drink, making sure our glasses were never empty.

"Oh, can I get some ice?"

"No, ma'am, I don't recommend. Not good for tourists," he responded, handing me the somewhat cold margarita that was so strong my face winced.

"Okay, no worries, thanks for letting me know," which I googled later to remind Sel to not drink the tap water either.

"Ah, good idea coming to India Sel. Gosh, I'm happy," I said to her, as the sun was sizzling on our skin, drying the ocean water from the last dip.

"Thanks for coming with me, Katie, I love it here too." I was so content in that moment, remembering the importance of travel, to adventure somewhere different and to experience different cultures. Not for escapism but for exploration, and to learn more about the world and other people in it. *But boy, did I miss opening my mouth in the shower.*

25

Markets

After a few days, we were happy to take a break from the sea, sun and salt, and looked at our list of things we wanted to do. We had drunk all day at the Mayan Beach Club, we had eaten all day and swam with other tourists at Calamari and we had dined at Olive, watching another perfect sunset, always finding ourselves in awe of the vibrant hues of the sky and how it cast a shimmering path across the ocean. We had tried nearly all the foods the guys had recommended and drank our bodyweight in Cabo and pineapple juice. Another wonderful recommendation of theirs.

"What about the Mapusa Markets?" Sel asked. While I wasn't a fan of markets, I thought it was something a little different.

"I did want to get a gift for Gary, Ads and the family," I said. Our hotel organized a driver to take us and told us he would wait until we were ready to leave.

"We might be two hours though?" I said, slightly concerned he would leave us, but he shook his head sideways, which we had now learned was the cultural way of expressing, *yes, sure* and *no worries.*

We made our way past jeweller after jeweller, side stalls and alleyways and came across an open area full of different colors and smells, and women. Click click click. There were older women, their hair tied in grey buns, with bright saris, sitting on low chairs under colorful umbrellas. They all looked tired, whether from the heat or from sitting there all day, I didn't know. All the women were only selling fruit and vegetables for some reason, and we began buying some on the way. There were bananas, sweet potato, pumpkin, papaya and pineapple.

"Danyavaad," one woman said, taking my rupees and smiling, her head bobbing from side to side. I noticed her short nails and about fifteen bangles on each of her slim, wrinkly wrists.

"I wonder why all the younger women tend to have their hair in low ponytails and the older women tend to have their hair in low buns?" I asked Sel, wondering if that's just how it was, or if there was a reason. Like, if there was a reason everyone seemed to be dripping in gold. *Was it real gold?*

As we kept walking, I noticed there were now tubs of beautiful colors. As we got closer, I saw it was colorful rocks. I smelt it.

"Incense?" I asked, looking at the gentlemen who nodded. He picked up another rock from another tub, smelt it and held it toward me to smell too, naturally I bobbled my head back in response. The other tubs were filled with cloves, dry orange things, star aniseed, pepper and other spices I wasn't able to decipher. The smells were aromatic, like nothing I had experienced before.

A sheer panic engulfed me as I looked around ready to pass the incense to Sel and couldn't see her close by. I caught a glimpse of her curly brown hair in the distance entering another area.

"Sel," I yelled, no-one hearing me. The sound of my words being muffled by the crowd of people everywhere. She heard me though, somehow. Her innocent face lighting up as she pointed toward sweets in a bakery.

"They are like some fancy award-winning bakery," she said, as I caught up and she began ordering one of everything. "Ooooh what's that?" she asked the lady, who was pointing at small golden looking things with dents in them.

"Kulkuls," she said, "tasty." Sel nodded, giving her a thumbs up and then moving onto something else. The lady handed us both little tastes of them and other sweets, enjoying watching our eyes light up every time we tried something new.

"They are a bit sweet," I said to Sel, who didn't seem to care.

We were in an inside area, which seemed to have semi closed. There were tables with ancient-looking sewing machines and multiple bags of flowers, almost the size of me.

"Where is everyone?" Sel asked a woman behind a glass counter, where it seemed she was selling pickles and chutneys. She appeared younger than most women who were around, her face youthful and slim, her gold nose ring catching the light as she spoke.

"Most people around here finish at two pm, the early morning is the busiest. Or come on a Friday, it's packed then," she said. "Would you like to try some chutney?"

"Are they spicy?" I responded, peering into the glass jars, also seeing containers of dried fish. She shook her head, getting out multiple pop-sticks and opening jars.

"This is a mango pickle," she said, handing it to us, which Sel instantly didn't like. I did. It was a sweet, but sour, a salty taste with a hint of spice. My mouth watered. She gave me a few to try, quickly realizing I didn't know what I picked when I decided to buy two jars full. She told me about the salt fish, and how they pickle it. It was her family's recipe and business, and she helped out a few days a week, but generally lived in Mumbai.

"Oh, Katie, it's been over two hours, we better get back," Sel said, as she waved goodbye to the lady and we walked back the way we came, through stalls of clothes and shoes, hopeful we were going the right way.

"There he is," Sel pointed. And sure enough, the driver was standing exactly where we left him, glad we didn't forget what he looked like or he forgot what we did. Although, that would have been impossible given we were the only foreigners in sight.

For the hour's drive back, we sat in silence, probably for different reasons. I could see Sel looking out the window, every now and then, munching on the sweets she bought, offering them to me and the driver. I, on the other hand, was processing the experience, thinking about the woman I saw sleeping on the chair next to the old sewing machine, about the young woman selling pickles for her family and the train ride she would be taking back to Mumbai any day now. *It's all luck really, isn't it?* Where we are born. The family we were born into. Only really being able to play the cards we were dealt.

We had originally planned to stay around the northern beach area in Goa for two whole weeks to party, however the more we were talking with people, the more we realized there were so many parts of Goa to explore.

"Want to go to that Fontainhas area those guys mentioned?" I asked Sel a week in, as we were on yet another day bed by the ocean drinking another Cabo and pineapple juice. She pulled out her phone and began searching.

"I mean, why not, it's an hour away, though I wouldn't mind a couple more days by the beach before we go to Kerala," she said. I agreed. We planned to check out of the hotel the next day and head to the Fontainhas area. We found a bed and breakfast run by a husband and wife, which had breakfast included and booked it, excited for the next adventure.

26

Fontainhas

The drive into Panaji was all traffic, however once the traffic subsided and we were in the Fontainhas area, we could feel the change in atmosphere. The houses began lining up and the colors grew brighter. The road turned into pavement and as we passed quaint streets, I could see green gardens and cobblestones. There were cute cafes and an abundance of tourists.

"I wonder what that is?" Sel asked, as we passed what looked like a Christian temple; a ceramic Jesus-like statue within glass embodiment on the side of a building.

"Welcome," the husband said when we arrived, our large suitcases being carried in by the taxi driver. The husband was much taller than usual. He had a round belly that made him look bigger than he may have been. His once-black hair brushed back was streaked with grey. He had a stern look, although he spoke kindly. I watched as one of the young men who worked at the bed and breakfast nodded at the husband and disappeared with our bags, assumingly taking them to the room.

"Where are you from?" he asked, curiously, requesting our passports and gesturing for us to sit down on creaky wooden furniture. The young man appeared again with two cold drinks, which appeared to be papaya juice. I had grown fond of its unique taste and thick texture when juiced.

It reminded me of cantaloupe.

"I'm from the US, and Sel is from Portugal," I said. He looked impressed with Sel.

"You will find it very beautiful here. There is a famous bakery around the corner that does tasty Portuguese tarts. This Latin, or French, or Portuguese corner – whichever you want to call it – has quite a European twist to it," he said, pulling out a brochure after he had written our details in his book and taken photos of our passports. He unfolded the brochure, revealing a map with points of interest and places to go. He began circling areas and pointing toward different directions. I smiled and nodded, but found myself not listening, instead marvelling at the interior of the property, the wooden panels and Portuguese art around the room.

"Is that a tour?" I interrupted him, looking outside and seeing a group of people walking together.

"Yes, they do walking tours around the town as well. You might like that. There's lots of history about this particular area of Goa. There is another one this evening, about four pm I think," he said. I looked at Sel, who nodded. We had both grown to say less and less words to each other. The husband, Ronald, allowed us to check in early and after a quick freshen up, we strolled to the nearest cafe for some food, marvelling at the architecture and the beauty of the area, taking photos wherever I could, enjoying the mixture of tourists and pedestrians in the shot. We booked the walking tour at the cafe for four pm, and I was excited to see what other things I would get images of.

"I think I'm going to head back to the hotel and relax, is that okay?" I asked Sel. She seemed hesitant at first, but then nodded. I realized we hadn't had a proper break from each other in the week we had been here and needed some time alone. I wanted to have time to check in with Gary, and with John, which is exactly what I did when I got back to the hotel. Gary shared how the packing was going, and how intense it was trying to make decisions on the restaurant without visually seeing it first. John said the gallery was quiet and jokingly wondered why he had been paying me so much. I could hear he was bored, and maybe even lonely without us.

The meeting area for the walking tour was only two minutes away from the bed and breakfast, and I headed there about five minutes earlier in case for some reason I got lost and laughed when I saw Sel on the way. She was holding a bag, that looked like oil was seeping through it.

"The Portuguese tarts here are pretty amazing, they remind me of home," she said, holding out the bag toward me, as soon as she saw me. It was the tantalizing sugar hit I needed. "You okay?" she asked, probably realizing it had also been the first time we had actively spent time apart.

"Yes, I just wanted some time to check in with Gary and John. I just needed some time alone," I said, linking my arm around her's and now walking closer than I had ever this entire trip. She held my linked arm with her other one, like we were an old married couple walking down the road, although we had a spring in our step. We saw the tour sign from afar, looking at a small group of multicultural people from all over the world form a small circle. It was the first time I had heard accents other than Indian, German and Russian ones by the beach, and it was nice. There were also people who had flown from other parts of India to meet their family or friends who were in Goa.

The tour began with the guide introducing herself, explaining she was a local who grew up there, and then asked everyone to say their name, where they were from and what brought them to the Fontainhas area. Many had come for weddings, some to see family and some were just here on a holiday, like us. When the tour started, I began taking notes:

- Oldest Latin quarter in Asia

- In the fourteenth century it was Muslim ruled

- Was governed by Portuguese rulers even once the British left the rest of India

- Goa has the same postcode as research stations in Antarctica
- Some of the first female scientists to participate in Antarctic expeditions were Indian, breaking stereotypes and paving the way for future generations of female scientists and researchers
- Houses are one hundred and fifty to two hundred years old
- The area was a UNESCO world heritage site

"Be present, you're missing things by writing it," Sel said, tugging at my arm as we turned the corner and saw the alleyway transform into the most picturesque old town in Europe. "Oh, this is that famous bakery." I took a photo and put my phone away, following the guide's instructions to go inside and take a seat. Shortly after, sweets were passed around with perad and other Indian sweets cut into small pieces for all to try before heading to a Greek-style hostel, where they played Goan music for us, while we drank an awful-tasting red drink, kokum juice, that I couldn't tell whether it was sweet, sour or savory.

We found dinner on the way home, feeling intoxicated even though we hadn't had a sip of alcohol, then lay in bed in wonder, talking about our favorite things from the day and planning what we would do the next. *What an amazing world we live in.*

27

Kerala

I fell in love with Goa. Some of the views were the most beautiful I'd ever seen before, with the ocean and the radiant sunsets. I had never seen sunsets burn so red and illuminate the sky with so much orange, or experienced ocean water that felt so warm without harsh waves. The sun also never seemed to set at the horizon, but disappear just above it, like it got lost in a mist or clouds. *Or was it pollution?* I was sad to leave the ocean but was looking forward to the jungle and a different environment.

There was only one flight from Goa to Kochi International Airport. It was an hour long, but for some reason the flight wasn't until nine pm. We had to check out of our hotel in the morning and had our bags, so after wandering around trying not to get sweaty, and as the sun set for the last time by the ocean, we got to the airport early … and waited.

"You're kidding me," Sel said, as she received a text that the flight was delayed by an hour. The heat, the crowds and not eating well for the last few days had taken a toll on our patience.

"That's not too bad," I said, pulling whatever enthusiasm I could find. I rubbed her shoulder to provide some comfort, not wanting our moods ruined. We found a quiet spot in a coffee shop, plugged in our phones to charge and grabbed a hot chocolate, each of us taking turns to man our carry-on bags while the other went to the bathroom or for a stroll. Selina fell asleep on the chair, but I couldn't do it. There was always a part of me that was worried someone would steal my phone or my bag. I still felt that way going to the bathroom on a flight too, although nothing had ever happened to me.

When our flight finally boarded, everyone rushed. Sel and I stood back, tired and grumpy, not understanding why people would rush for allocated seats. *Is it because they were concerned they wouldn't get any space in the overhead cabins?* We watched everyone push, like it may take off without them on it. Sel and I didn't say anything, we didn't even look at each other this time, we were at a point of mutual understanding and ready to see each other on the other side.

We took our time getting off the plane and getting our luggage. It was close to midnight and the positive about it was that the airport was empty … ish and we didn't need to go through any customs. We slowly followed the arrows and people from the flight to the exit. This time, our sign was huge; a solid A2 piece of paper with our names as big as a 'welcome home' sign friends or family might make for loved ones returning home after years abroad. It pulled at my heart strings.

"How small was our last sign compared to this?" Sel laughed. I was glad her humor was back, even if it was for only a moment. We walked up to the guy holding the sign. He looked to be about thirty-eight, with a cheeky smile, one you can instantly trust. He had a warmth about him, a sweetness.

"Selina and Katelyn?" he asked. We nodded. "Come with me," he said, taking both of our bags. The words were abrupt and demanding, but the way he said it was soft and gentle. We were definitely getting used to the care we received here. "We will go to your driver."

"You're not the driver?" I asked.

"No, I'm the retreat manager."

"You drove an hour here just to get us?" Sel asked, astonished. That seemed like a lot of time. I guess we were paying sixty Euros one way.

"Yes, we want to make sure you arrive safely," he responded. It was definitely not what we were expecting and felt it was such a kind touch. At the same time, I received a message from the booking team.

Did Suresh pick you up from the airport? He should be holding a sign – it read. I showed Sel my phone, and she raised her eyebrows, nodding in appreciation for it too. I responded that we were safe and with him.

There wasn't much we could see on the drive as it was dark outside. There were lots of closed shops and dark streets, at one stage driving through what seemed like a rainforest, with nothing around except trees. *Could I have done this myself?* There was every possibility they could have hacked the retreats system, found our names, come to the airport and now they were kidnapping us, taking us out into the wilderness to be sold or have our things stolen. The thoughts came, fastened when we stopped, and then slowed when Suresh handed us two cold bottles of water he purchased from the side of the road.

"You must be so thirsty," he said. "Please, feel free to sleep. We will have you at the retreat soon where we will have some food waiting for you." I wiggled my hips to the right and leant against the window on the left of me, closing my eyes.

I naturally woke when we stopped at the retreat. The taxi driver took out our bags, shook Suresh's hand and got back in the car. I reached for my money, but he shook his head.

"We will deal with that later, don't worry," he said, "come with me." We followed him through the front entrance, a large wooden-framed door into a small waiting area of couches and wooden artwork hanging from the walls. As we walked through, there was glass beneath us, creating a fake pond, and when we looked up, there was an actual pond with fish swimming in it. There was also the sound of water from a fountain I wasn't able to see. We continued following Suresh through a kitchen area, where a tall man came from around the corner, his hands straight by his sides, as he gently bowed his head as we passed. A gentle giant, one you didn't hear walk past, he would glide. He was soft spoken and very courteous and caring. He led us to an outdoor table with a placemat and napkin opened out on it, and cutlery perfectly in place. He brought out a glass of water and a fruit bowl.

"Eat," he said, pointing. "Is there anything else you would like?" We shook our heads. They spoke to each other in something that wasn't Hindi. It sounded melodic. It wasn't words, it was as if they were communicating in sounds. We both sat eating our fruit salad, looking around, but not being able to see much past the wooden table and a small balcony bordered with plants and a hammock hung within it. It was silent, besides the sounds of insects in the distance. Suresh waited patiently for us to finish our fresh fruit juice and fruit salad before showing us to our rooms. We decided to have separate rooms because it was our first time travelling together and wanted the space to relax whenever we needed to, after we'd just spent a solid two weeks together.

"I put you next to each other," Suresh said as we followed him back past the glass floor and up a steep spiralling staircase, "we have you in this one … just let me know if you swap." The rooms were different but neither of us minded. Our balconies attached which was helpful as well. It's like we were in the same room, without having to sleep right next to each other.

"The ayurvedic doctor is coming tomorrow if you would like to see him? Yoga is at seven-thirty am so don't worry about starting tomorrow as it's early, and treatments will usually be around eleven am, and two or three pm, but we will give you more information tomorrow. Breakfast is usually at eight-thirty am, lunch at one pm and dinner at seven pm. You can get snacks and tea around four pm if you wish as well, but if you need anything, Rajan will be here to look after you, as will I, and Jithin as well, who you will meet tomorrow. Many of us live on site, so you can call or text me at any time if you need anything. Jithin does the tours and water sports," he added. He waited a little while to see if we had any questions, but as we were only politely smiling and staring at him, he bobbled his head side to side and turned to leave.

"Night, babe," I said to Sel, slowly closing my door.

"Night, hun. Will text you when I'm up in the morning," she said, closing hers too. I gave the room a quick glance, checking for mould and insects under the pillows and other blankets. It was a habit I didn't know where I'd picked up from, but when I was satisfied, I took off my clothes and went straight to sleep. The rest, I could deal with tomorrow.

28

Retreat

With the exhaustion from the day before, I realized I hadn't put my alarm on when I went to sleep, but naturally woke up to the hum of birds and the sun beaming through the windows. It had gotten warm too. Looking around I could see I had kicked my blankets off the bed.

As I slowly blinked my eyes open, there was a moment of confusion. *Where was I? Where's Sel?* Then I remembered I was in the middle of nowhere in Kerala and she was next door or maybe at breakfast. I could hear chatter in the distance, but it wasn't loud. I patted around the bed for my phone and saw I had left it on the side table by the bed. It lit up from a message that was received.

It was Sel, telling me she had headed down for breakfast. There were emails requesting I reviewed all the places we went to in Goa, and there was a message from Ads and Mom checking in. I didn't bother to open any other social media apps, I wanted to see where I was.

It was five past eight am, and though I still felt tired, I was ready to explore. I dug through my suitcase to find a loose linen dress to throw on and unlocked the door to the balcony. Wow, I was instantly enthralled. I ran to my bed to grab my camera, even though I had enough time to take photos while I was here. Click click click. I knew there was something about the first moment you lay your eyes on beauty like this. I wanted to remember this feeling when I looked back at the photos.

The air was still, but thick, far from the cool sea breeze we were used to. The wooden balcony was spacious, with two intricately woven wooden seats and a glass table in the centre. The view was of the vast river that surrounded us, stretching endlessly from left to right. Directly opposite there was dense and lush greenery. *What animals lived in there?* The more I looked, the more I saw. There were spiders weaving delicate webs, ants busying themselves and butterflies fluttering around gracefully.

It was the splash into the water that brought me back to reality. I went back inside to wash my face and prepare myself for any other guests who were staying here. Following the smell of spices, I made my way to where we had our fruit salad last night, retracing my way down the steep spiral staircase and across the glass floor passing through the kitchen area. The dining area opened to the same breathtaking view of the river from my balcony, stretching endlessly into the horizon. The water was still, creating a mirror-like surface that reflected the dense jungle opposite us. "Morning," I said to anyone I walked past, wooden tables arranged to the left and right of the alfresco area, with vibrant green leaves in every corner. There was a hammock gently swaying, cradling someone engrossed in a book.

"Morning, Katie," Sel said, waving at me. She looked fresh, like we hadn't transited the exact same way last night. I took a seat next to her, my gaze not leaving the river views.

"It's stunning, isn't it?" she said, her eyes following where mine were. I nodded.

"The place is amazing, another five stars for that traveller," I said to Sel. Rajan had started bringing out my breakfast, beginning with a freshly squeezed fruit juice and fruit salad, then three bowls of different types of curries – spinach, chickpeas and potatoes – followed up with what looked like rice noodles, only remembering then that this was a vegan retreat and I no longer had the choice of eggs for breakfast, or meat for lunch.

"Tea or coffee?" he asked.

"Masala tea please." It was one of the things I had fallen in love with in Goa; the aromatic spices mixed with black tea. I found it odd that we called it 'chai' back home and learned that chai was just 'tea' in Hindi. *Did everyone know we were just saying 'tea' in Hindi when ordering chai?*

Selina told me the doctor had come early to see other guests and that her appointment was at nine am, with mine being after. I was excited to hear what the doctor would ask, or what I would learn, as I truly had no idea what I was doing there, nor had any expectations.

"Do you have any issues you would like to be treated while you are here?" the doctor asked.

"Not really, I think bloating is the main thing, but that's when I eat bad food. Otherwise, I am here for general health and stress relief," I said. She went through a health checklist, asked about any life changes and took my blood pressure.

"You're moving cities? That has to be hard," she said.

"I'm moving back home, it's what I know. It'll be fine," I said, as I brushed it off in that moment, but realized I hadn't lived in our family home since I was a teenager, surely that might not be as easy as I initially imagined. I haven't had to see my old childhood things all the time or needed to rely on Mom. Now I was going to move back in with Gary, who I might be dating. Suddenly, it did start to feel a little wild.

The doctor set me up with a standard plan. I would have a head massage in the morning for five days, and a full body massage and steam in the evening for five days. Then the following five days would be a different kind of head massage in the morning, and a detox treatment in the evening. I didn't realize it was going to be two treatments in a day, plus yoga and three sit-down meals in the restaurant. I wondered where I would find the time to actually explore the area.

"Your medicine will start at six pm this evening, and you will also have one at six am starting tomorrow," she continued.

"What medicine?" I asked, being someone that didn't even take pain killers for headaches.

"To help with the detoxification process. I have only prescribed two different medicines for you. Your morning one will be a sweet tea-like drink, which will help with your digestion, and the evening one will help relax the body for sleep." I asked to take a photo of the actual words she was writing, as I was aware she was simplifying it for me. I wanted to be able to google what it all was later.

She asked if I had any more questions, and when I said *no*, she nodded and looked at one of the young women by the door. She walked closer to me and gestured it was time to leave, by bowing her head and making an outward motion with her hand.

29

Familiar

From what I understood of the treatments, which was very little, it turned out to be very different to what I thought. I stood at the front of the retreat, where I saw people coming and going during the day for treatments, until a short young woman came to get me. She was maybe in her early to mid-twenties, with big curious eyes and a small red bindi on her forehead. She asked me to follow her for my first treatment. The room we entered was small, there was a massage table in the middle, a small shelf to the right and a wooden cupboard on the left-hand side. There was deep relaxation music playing.

"Please remove your top and bra, miss," she said politely, her eyes not moving away as she waited patiently.

"Oh, all of it?" I confirmed. She nodded. I slowly removed the top I was wearing and my bra while she moved a wooden box between us. *What was the box for?* Once I had followed her instructions and stood bare-breasted, covering myself as best I could with my hands, she placed a disposable cover on it and pointed for me to sit down. I followed her instructions, covering my breasts as my body faced away from her. She removed my hair tie and started massaging my scalp and neck. I could feel the warm ghee dripping from my scalp down the nape of my neck, while she rhythmically pressed into the area. I closed my eyes to fully savor the sensation and the aroma. She then asked me to lie down on the table, as I heard her heat a pot. She began massaging my face and temples and then angled my face up, then dropped warm oil into my nose. It reminded me of butter. I could feel it travel up my sinuses and swallowed what had begun creeping down my throat.

"Sit up," she instructed. "Breathe quickly." I did, faster and faster, until she told me to slow down. She put cotton balls in my ears and nose and told me not to remove them for fifteen minutes, and to be back at two pm for my next treatment.

I went straight to my room, a peaceful sensation rushing over me but also curiosity. I found the Wi-Fi password before laying on my bed to check the screenshot I took of the doctor, and then googled what I had just experienced.

Nasyam – the administration of medicated oils or powders through the nostrils, beneficial for any mental concerns, sinus issues, headaches and supports the respiratory system.

I read it, realizing I probably should have done more research on the vegan, treatment-filled retreat I would be doing in the middle of nowhere. The butter-like fluid was uncomfortable in my sinuses, and I decided to sit up, hoping that it would just slowly run its course due to gravity. I waited and then I lay down again, confused as to whether I found this enjoyable or put it down to healing.

I napped before lunch but intuitively woke up because I was hungry. I hadn't eaten since eight-thirty am that morning and didn't want to leave it too close to my second treatment. Sel wasn't down in the alfresco area yet but I noticed there were a few other travellers sitting at the table, one feeling familiar before properly seeing her.

I walked past her to take a seat and watched as her dark curly hair turned as she did.

"Felicity?" I asked. She quickly looked toward me, firstly with confusion and then pure delight.

"Oh … umm …" she started, knowing she was trying to remember my name.

"Katelyn, from New York," I stepped in to assist.

"Yesss, that's right. Oh my God, what are you doing here?" she excused herself from her friend, apologizing first but then springing up to give me a hug. Her embrace was warm, exciting and nostalgic. She turned to the girl she was sitting with, a slim woman with long brown hair, her skin pale. "Etelia, this is Katelyn. She helped me with directions in New York – gosh – over a year ago now? and that's really all," she laughed. Etelia nodded her head shyly, with a quiet *hi*, that I think escaped her mouth, but I couldn't be sure. "How are you?"

"Gosh, I think I last saw you in Brooklyn? It's a wild story. I was so taken by you and your adventures that I travelled a little bit. I went to Iceland and London, spent time with my estranged family in Scotland and ended up living in Hawaii for a year. I've decided to move back to Manhattan but a friend of mine and I decided to travel through India first, before I move back," I quickly said, summarizing what I could in the moment. There was so much more to share, but I didn't know how.

"I do remember seeing you in Brooklyn but can't remember what you told me. I think you had just broken up with your partner. Gosh, I'm glad you travelled though, what a different life you're living from when I saw you back then. How are you doing now?" she asked, putting her hand on my arm, the same act I did to Sel when I was at the airport. It comforted me.

"I'm doing good. Another life change, but I miss home," I said. "Sorry, I feel that was a bit of a dump."

"Don't be silly, I asked how you were and much prefer that than the standard, *yeah good*,"

"And you? How are you? What brings you to India?" I asked her.

"I had a wedding in Goa and I was going to go north, but there were a few security warnings so thought it may be safer to head south. Although now that I'm here, I feel it would have been fine. Here is beautiful though, so no regrets. Maybe I was meant to bump into you again." I agreed, on both parts. I had seen the alerts on the travel websites warning female travellers, but my experience was nothing like I had thought.

"You came by yourself?" I asked her, she nodded. I wondered if it wasn't for John, and Sel working at a backpacker's retreat, if I would have had the courage to do it on my own, like Felicity.

"Yes, everyone else went home after the wedding. The newlyweds continued travelling around India to see friends and family, but I wanted to do something a little out of the ordinary. I don't think anyone else would have been keen for this, if I'm being honest though," she laughed, "although, look at that." Her eyes travelled across the river again, just like mine had done this morning.

"How long are you here for?" I asked her.

"I have about four days to go, then back to Australia and back to work to save to travel again," she laughed. I could have kept talking to her for ages, but I didn't want to keep her from Etelia.

"Well, we have a few more days to catch up. Finish your conversation, and I'll see you at dinner?" Felicity nodded and hugged me again, before sitting back down. I found an empty seat with plates set up and Rajan began bringing out my food – or a feast to be correct; there were papadums, roti, three different types of curries again, a fruit salad.

"You have to tone down the food, Rajan, I can't eat that much," I kind of joked. He laughed and bobbled his head, and as he went inside, Sel walked out, with cotton buds in her ears and a slight look of disarray on her face.

"You did the nasayam?" I said, unable to hold a serious face. She nodded, sharing how maybe we needed to do some research before the next treatment as well. I shared how uncomfortable it made me feel, to have been so exposed without towels covering us. Sel didn't seem to mind that as much, she was comfortable with her body and skin, and I wondered if that was something I needed to work on about myself. I told Sel about Felicity, and how we met when she asked me for directions in New York, and it was the reason I walked into the travel agency in the first place. Then how I found the note in my pocket with the quote, and then also seeing her in Brooklyn, like each time something pivotal was going to happen, she was there.

"That's crazy, surely not a coincidence," she said. "Think it's a sign to go to Australia too? We are as close as we'll ever be to it." I wasn't sure if she was joking or not.

"No way John would let us," I said, looking at her, my mind not truly entertaining the idea surely it was too far away and too expensive. Sel shrugged and grabbed her phone, looking how far it was geographically.

"I mean, what's the harm in asking? It doesn't look toooo far," she said, zooming in and out of Google Maps and comparing where Honolulu was to Kerala … and then where Kerala was to Australia.

"There could be a direct flight. But hey, we have time to figure it out. We have another ten days here," Sel said confidently. I opened my photography schedule and didn't have another shoot for another four weeks in Hawaii. *Maybe timing-wise that would all work? Or were we just being a little crazy?*

30

Meditation

The afternoon treatment, which I decided to research before going into it, was actually called Abhyanga and Steam. It was a full-body massage with ayurvedic oils to nourish the body's tissue, followed by a steam bath to open up the pores and flush out impurities. I liked the sound of that and was ready when the time came for it.

I made my way back down to the front of the retreat, where my therapist was waiting.

"Hello, ma'am, my name is Anjali," her head bowed. "Everything off," she said, closing the door behind her.

"Underwear too?" I asked, feeling uncomfortable again. She nodded, and then took out a disposable G-string, tying the ends to make it fit. I slowly started undressing, folding everything into a box that was under the table. It felt so unusual to be bare like this, but I reminded myself *this is her job,* and she had seen everyone doing this multiple times a day. *Is it because of my western culture I feel this way?* She had me sit on the box again, covered by the disposable sheet, and began massaging my neck, covering me with ghee once more. The smell of it now felt familiar to me. She guided me to lay on the table, massaging the back of me first, from head to toe. I felt the sequences of her hands across my body, the grounding music playing in the background that gradually eased me into a state of deep relaxation. When I turned over, I heard her turn on gas, to heat something, *the steam bath?* I wondered what room it was in or where I would go after. Surprisingly, when she told me to get up for the steam, she walked me to the cupboard I had seen earlier. She opened the cupboard, fixed the height of the seat inside and had me sit in, my head poking out of a small circular hole. It felt like a magician's box awaiting a trick. I could feel the heat come through from behind me, filling up the small cupboard box I was sitting in, thinking how the term 'steam bath' seemed to promise a more luxurious experience. I sat there for fifteen minutes, sweating. Moments of relaxation flooded me, but so did moments of anxiety and feeling claustrophobic. *Would I get stuck in there? Could I get burned?* When it was over, she wrapped me in a sheet, gave me my clothes and told me not to shower for at least fifteen minutes.

When I got back to my room, I didn't know what to do. I was too oily to lie down and too bare to sit on the balcony with only a sheet wrapped around me. I decided to sit in silence, an unusual urge I've never felt the need to do.

I sat on the rug at the base of my bed, my legs crossed and eyes closed. I could smell the ghee on my body and feel it on my skin. I could hear the wind, and the birds, cars from the front of the retreat, a tuk tuk here and there. I listened to my breath, and how my stomach rose and dropped with each one. I saw black, darkness. Then I saw Mark. I saw the life we lived, and how it all ended in Hawaii, replaying moments of me sobbing on the beach in darkness, and I seemed to be watching myself from above. As if I was out of my body. I saw the beautiful life I had been living in Hawaii, and the face of Gary and my family. Goosebumps engulfed my body at the thought of living back in the Brooklyn house. I could see me and Gary in there, and I started to sob, tears falling from my eyes. It felt like a release; a release of emotions, neither good nor bad. I held those images in my mind and sobbed until I couldn't anymore, my eyes remaining closed, letting the tears stream softly from my eyes and drop onto my chest. It felt surreal, but with a knowing I was in the right place, doing what I was supposed to be doing and living the life I was meant to be living.

31

Knowing

At six pm, there was a knock at my door. I was freshly showered and lying in bed, pondering the meditation experience I'd had. Rajan was there, with a tray. He handed me something black; a bitter soup. I drank it, and then some warm water after. I looked back at the screenshot I took, then googled it again:

Thailam – sesame oil medicated with herbal mixes, works at the tissue level and can help maintain skin health and manage skin conditions. It's an antioxidant and anti-microbial.

I wondered if what I was reading was correct, but the doctor seemed to appreciate there was nothing specific I felt I needed. I continued to google the treatments I would have after five days, and the medication I would receive in the morning.

Kashayam – a herbal drink to boost immunity.

Shirodhara – a continuous stream of warm herbal oil being poured onto the forehead, which is deeply relaxing.

Elakizhi – massaging with small linen bags filled with heated herbal leaves, promoting better circulation.

I spent the entire hour before dinner googling these ayurvedic therapies, the history and how modern medicine uses it now, and wanted to truly embrace the experience. But I was excited for dinner to come around and to see Sel and Felicity, and whoever else may have checked into the retreat.

I went down to the alfresco area and as soon as I saw Sel, I wrapped my arms around her. I missed the infectious energy she radiated, the way her presence always had me giggling around her. I realized my pace was slower without her, I naturally recoiled into my room and rested alone, maybe because of the fast-paced last two weeks or the feeling of being relaxed in this new magical retreat. Her hair was damp, and she was wrapped in a towel.

"What have you been doing?" I asked her, looking around to see the friends she was with. There was an older man from the UK, his grey wet hair pushed up into a ponytail, still slightly dripping.

"I got bored after the treatment. I saw people swimming from the balcony and came down to join them," she said, her eyes wide with excitement. There were a couple of steps from the alfresco area down into the river, and a small floating jetty that I hadn't noticed before. An older man and his daughter were on it, he was sitting with his legs dangling in the water and she was lying in the sunshine. Her eyes closed and she was smiling. "Apparently, there are snakes in the water," Sel added, which completely removed any ounce of interest I had to get in now.

"Well, that's a no from me then," I said, looking back to the water noticing it wasn't clear after a few feet, imagining if all the water was gone, what animals were swimming in there. I could deal with fish, and that's about it. The water was slightly moving, which was good, but it was deep, and I didn't do well if I couldn't see the bottom. The grey topknot guy dove back in, the water splashing on the young girl on the floating jetty, she screamed with glee, and I watched him swim out.

"Get in," Sel said, nodding her head in the direction they were all in. I shook mine.

"He's not even standing, I can tell," I said.

"Yeah, it's deep. There are steps at the beginning and then they just disappear." Sel told me about how the water felt soft against her skin, and how she felt energized being in it, like a natural cleanser.

"This place is interesting, isn't it? I had the urge to meditate for the first time in ages, and my visions were intense," I said. Sel and I had never talked about anything so deep and spiritual before. We had talked about our dreams and plans, or countries we wanted to travel to, but I hadn't realized beyond that moment it had never been about spirituality outside of, *do you think everything happens for a reason?*

"What do you think that means?" she asked, after I told her about the vision.

"I don't know, maybe nothing? I think I was just processing. The last year has been go, go, go, and I think I have pushed so much away, rather than actually thinking about it and reflecting on it."

Rajan came out and started putting plates and cutlery on the table, subtly telling us that dinner was ready. The ones that were swimming, including Sel, went to shower, while I joined other guests at the dining area. Felicity was sitting there, this time alone, reading her book. She put it down as she saw me approaching her.

"Aw, Felicity, how wild," I said to her again, still in awe to be seeing her. Her eyes closed as she nodded in agreeance, a calm exuding her.

"How do you like it here?" she asked, her gaze panning the river's length, the sun now slowly setting, changing the colors of the sky surrounding us.

"Love it. I actually meditated before and it reminded me of how little I slow down," I paused, "I mean not slow down like sitting and watching Netflix to turn the world off, but to sit in silence and listen to what's happening within me." She was nodding again, in agreeance.

"Yes, this place does bring it out of you. I have been trying to stay off my phone too but finding it hard to disconnect completely."

"We are so addicted to them, aren't we," I said in frustration.

"We need to be, it's how our society works. I think there is a balance we need to learn though. I only find it when I travel, which also isn't great. I need to learn a trick for normal life."

"What do you do in your normal life?" I asked her, realizing I actually knew nothing about this carefree traveller, who seems to be everywhere all the time, experiencing, nothing seemingly tying her down.

"I have an engineering background but had my own realisation around the time I met you. I had given so much of my life to large corporations and started my own consulting business so I could get more balance. It's been the best thing I ever did."

"Do you have a partner, are you married?" I asked.

"I'm currently single, but I have met someone wonderful recently. We'll see how it goes. I'm a bit of a wild card, I don't feel normal," she laughed, her laughter lighting me up as well.

"And you're in Australia? I can't remember where though …"

"Little old Perth, the opposite side of the country to Sydney," she said. "It's one of the most isolated cities in the world but I love it there. I love going back to the place where I know nearly every nook and cranny. I love the weather. I love knowing where my friends are and seeing my family. It's special."

"I love that. I'm moving back to New York for the same reason. I feel I spent the last year running … well – maybe not running but avoiding my feelings. Now, being here, I'm so appreciative of it all. but I'm also so ready to be with my friends and family again." I had a deep sense of knowing while I was saying it. We turned to look at everyone coming back from their showers, their hair wet and faces fresh, wearing clean clothes, clearly pulled straight out of a suitcase, the fabric still marked with creases.

"You're Felicity?" asked Sel, breaking the silence as she arrived. Felicity nodded, her relaxed eyes cast low but her grin stretching across her face revealing her front teeth. "Did Katie tell you we wanted to come to Australia?"

"I was getting there," I laughed, looking embarrassingly at Felicity, playfully rolling my eyes.

"Oh my gosh, please come. It's a beautiful place. It's quiet but there's some beautiful things to do in nature. It's still a five-hour flight from Sydney, but if you have the time and money, it's worth it. You can stay with me for a few days too."

Sel and I looked at each other, both thinking the exact same thing. *YOLO?*

32

Journey

We called John the next day, to see how far we could push it.

"I mean, he needs us, remember," Sel said, before calling. It reminded me of being a kid and having to call your parents to ask for permission to do something, except now we were in our mid-thirties and had a great relationship with this man who is really our boss. But I had done a big favor for him for an entire year, even though, I also kind of didn't, really.

"Girls, just go. Enjoy yourselves. I've been fine. You've done so well automating everything, Katie. When will you be back?"

"I have a shoot in four weeks' time, so I have to be back in three weeks at the very latest. It will throw off timing with how long I get at home in New York before Gary arrives, but that's not really a big deal."

Sel also got the thumbs up from the hostel she works at, and we got to booking our trip to Australia. It felt surreal.

"Perth is in the middle of nowhere, do we skip it and go straight to Sydney?"

"We get free accommodation in Perth though, and it looks to be the easiest flight from Kochi?" We played paper, scissors, rock and booked it. We flew from Kochi to KL, then KL to Perth. We would stay five days in Perth and fly to Sydney for five days.

"Should we go up to Cairns, and see the Great Barrier Reef?" Sel asked. Everything looked so close on the map, but the distances were much further away then we could actually fathom.

"Where does it end though?" I asked. "Do we just head over to New Zealand then as well?" I was frustrated, we both were, but the moment we looked at each other, we diffused ourselves and laughed.

"Let's just do Perth and Sydney? It's easy to fly back to Hawaii from Sydney. That makes sense. The rest will become too much I think." We both agreed. Felicity was just as excited as we were, planning what we would do between eating and treatments. It reminded me of when I was in Iceland with the Australian girls, and I booked a flight to London with them. The way that everything just works out. *Should I get in contact with them?*

Our days were the same, every morning started with a knock at my door at six am for the kashayam followed by seven am yoga, the only thing changing being the deeper connection we had with the people that worked there, ourselves, each other and the place. There was always a rotation with people leaving and new people arriving. The conversations repeated themselves. Some people I would connect with more than Sel, and vice versa. There were moments I wouldn't spend any time with Sel at all because she wanted to go to the close-by towns and temples with the other guests, and there were times we would sit together and chat, alone, just the two of us. I also asked the staff if I could take photos of Sel having treatments and provide the retreat with images for their website which they happily agreed to, allowing me to also expand my portfolio.

One evening after taking photos of Sel, I strolled by my usual therapy room and saw Anjali applying a reddish paste to one of the guest's palms. Anjali was focused, her hand slowly gliding creating intricate geometric patterns. I knocked on the door and asked if it was alright to take photos, which they agreed to. The closer I was to take photos, the more I could smell the delicate scent of herbs. Anjali explained that mehndi, which

I later found out was more commonly known as henna, was a body art used during religious or cultural celebrations and applied mostly to the hands or the feet. It was made from the leaves of the henna plant, and she explained to us how it's left on until it dries like clay and peels off, darkening before slowly fading away again. When Anjali was done with the other guest, she happily did mine too. I watched her, in amazement, at how the patterns naturally flowed from her, and listened while she talked about how she was an artist as well, selling paintings on Instagram to help support her family with dreams of travelling around the world. It was a moment I felt truly connected to this retreat and the people I had met here.

Sel and I also explored outside of the retreat as much as we could, taking a day trip with a guide into the jungle to bird watch one day, where we saw a tribe living in solitude. On another day, we went into Munnar, something that John told us we couldn't miss. Munnar was breathtaking. The ferocity of the great big mountains and the quieter valleys layered against each other like something from a utopian film. We tasted tea, touched tea, smelt tea and bought tea, and then went to a spice plantation where they showed us all the different plants and trees, and all the unspoken benefits from the spices. The fig trees felt surreal to me, like something from *Lord of the Rings*. On the day trip days, we'd miss out on lunch or a treatment, but worth it to explore more of Kerala.

By the end of the two weeks, I felt comfortable in my own skin. It was an empowering feeling being nude for my treatments. I became used to looking at my naked body and had such a profound appreciation for it. I might not have looked any different, but I felt different. I felt calmer, more present and lighter. My skin glowed, my jaw wasn't tense, my shoulders fell just a little bit lower, and the daily yoga had made me more flexible. I also felt a deep connection to the retreat and the people I had met.

India stole my heart, and I loved every moment discovering it.

33

Perth

"Did you think we were going to be in Australia when we started talking about this trip?" Sel asked me as were about to descend into Perth.

"Not in a million years," I said, my eyes peering out of the window as the coastline skimmed across the blue waters, the city getting closer and closer while the plane manoeuvred for landing. We had been travelling for ten hours by this point, leaving Kochi airport which flew direct to Kuala Lumpur airport.

"Is anything in an airport actually authentic?" Sel asked curiously, looking at the chicken rice counter during our layover in KL. "And does an airport transit count as visiting a place if you try something authentic while there?"

"Surely, they would need to somewhat be, like how we have ahi tuna just about everywhere. It's more or less the same really, right?" I said, not sure of my response but feeling it made sense. Sel lined up for chicken rice, but kaya bread was drawing me in. It looked like chunks of sugary butter between bread, and tea. I loved tea. In fact, I had missed 'normal' tea since spending time in Scotland.

"That, now?" Sel asked judgementally, disapproving of my right to eat sugary goodness even though she was the sugar fiend between the two of us. We had noodles on the plane and the thought of more savory food was making me nauseous, that or I think my body needed the energy hit. That's all we did in the airport for the entire two hours; eat and drink, until we boarded the next four-and-a-half hour flight to Perth. It was actually quite a simple flight, although they were both with budget airlines.

"I wonder if Felicity will meet us at the airport?" Sel asked on the final leg of the trip, also softly sharing with me that she hoped she wasn't intruding on me bonding with her alone. I reassured her she was adding to the experience, not taking anything away from it.

We disembarked into one of the smallest airports I had ever seen, made our way through immigration and customs and then to one of the four luggage carousels. "I cannot believe you guys are here!" Felicity yelled, her voice competing with others, still laced with delight, hugging us both with one of those hugs that make you feel warm and fuzzy on the inside.

"We were just saying as we were landing. We never imagined this would be in the mix," Sel said, as Felicity helped us with our bags and we strolled over to the parking lot, the sun piercing my skin.

It was a completely different experience leaving the airport in comparison to both New York and India – it was quiet and calm. As we drove to Felicity's place, I couldn't quite get over how flat the landscape was. "Look, I did tell you it was quiet here, but bear with me, I'll take you to mine to drop your bags off and freshen up, and we can go from there," she suggested, before asking more questions about the rest of our experience at the retreat.

Felicity, who we started nicknaming Flick, lived in a hipster-looking area called Leederville. It was bustling, and surrounded by cute cafes, bars and restaurants. She lived in a high-rise apartment, where the balcony overlooked the strip. It was a small one-bedroom apartment, but was perfectly curated inside, with white walls and beige furniture, along with statement art pieces. She had a desk in one corner, a couch in another and a bookshelf brimming with books too. It was clearly the space of a creative.

"Oh, Flick, are you sure you don't want us to stay at a hotel?" I asked, looking around and not being able to visually see where we were going to sleep.

"Don't be silly. I have two inflatable mattresses for you to sleep in the lounge. Honestly, it's only a few nights you're here. I mean, if you don't want to stay here, I won't be offended if you want to find a hotel though," she added, innocently and carefully.

"No, not at all. I love this!" said Sel. She was looking around at all her things, picking up books and flicking to a random page, then another random page, to go back to reading the blurb and putting it back. Flick had an exotic range of plants placed neatly around, some that looked like they'd been around for a long time, and some that were barely hanging on.

"Oh, look. Some of them don't like my travel plans," she chuckled when she noticed me looking at one. She leaned over to hold a dying leaf, "Sorry, bub," she said to it. We spent some time freshening up, putting snacks on the kitchen bench that we needed to try – Tim Tams, Arnott's Shapes, Jatts crackers, slices of tasty cheese – that was surrounded with white kitchen stools. Once I had showered and changed and it was Sel's turn freshen up, I joined Flick in the kitchen, sitting as she poured a glass of white wine.

"Oh! This must be your first drink in a while. Do you want to continue to be alcohol free?" she asked politely, stopping mid-pour. I shook my head insistently, ready for the golden liquid to touch my lips, romanticizing the smell and the taste in my head. I pushed Flicks elbow up gently, urging her to continue the pour. She chuckled. "I was thinking we could just do a local place for dinner tonight, and then I can take you to Kings Park. It's one of the prettier places to see the skyline. Is there anything in particular you wanted to do?" Flick asked. I started looking through my notes app, to see the things we had written down.

"Tell me if any of this is worth seeing, but we had written down Fremantle, Kings Park, beaches, Rottnest Island, Broome, Margaret River, Albany, Denmark, Ningaloo Reef and Esperance, the beach with the kangaroos on it."

"Well," she said, smiling with cheek, "that's not all going to happen in a few days, you will need another visit. Fremantle is easy enough for the day or dinner. We will do Kings Park tonight. We can definitely do the beaches, actually some of the nicer ones without waves are around Fremantle. Albany and Denmark are a six-ish-hour drive away. Ningaloo Reef is up north, on the way to Broome and that will take two days to drive, unless you want to fly but it's not cheap. Margaret River is down south. It's awesome, with the wineries and caves. Esperance also has beautiful beaches but it's an eight-hour drive away. It all depends how much you want to cram in or if you just want to enjoy?"

"Hmm, what do you recommend?"

"Well, you have four full days, right? We can go to Kings Park tonight after dinner and if you like the vibe we can hang about. Tomorrow, why don't we go to Rotto? Sorry, we Aussies shorten everything. 'Rotto' is short for Rottnest Island. The weather looks great and you'll get to see some cute island quokkas. Then we can decide what to do next. If you want a break from the beaches, we can visit the wineries in the south the next day."

"Sounds good," Sel yelled from the other room, clearly listening to our conversation, which was a relief because I would have felt bad making a decision on behalf of her. She came out dressed, her hair and make-up done like she had taken an hour getting ready, when it had been just fifteen minutes. *Everything was somehow always fifteen minutes?*

The evening was warm, a beautiful breeze flowing through the apartment with the doors and windows wide open. We finished our drinks, my camera in purse, strolled across the street for dinner – excited to eat meat for the first time in two weeks – and then Flick drove us to Kings Park.

We drove through the entry of the park, the tall trees uniformly lined to the left of us with different colored lights illuminating them, from the base of the trunk all the way to the highest tips of the canopy. I wound the window down in the hope I could take more of it in, and the scent of eucalyptus quickly filled the car. I closed my eyes, inhaling deeply. Flick drove around explaining that at four hundred hectares, which I googled converts to nine hundred and ninety acres, Kings Park was bigger than Central Park, it was one of the largest inner city parks in the world. She parked the car and we strolled through the war memorial, slowly reading the names of the fallen Australian soldiers during WWI, and then slowly followed the path leading us to the prettiest little skyline I had ever seen. I adjusted my camera's night lens and clicked away. There was something innocent about this place – how quiet and clean it was, how safe it felt and even how the air somehow felt nourishing. *Maybe there really was something special about this place?*

We found an empty area on the grass to sit with no-one close by, Flick pulling out a bottle of red wine and discreetly pouring it into three plastic cups. Sel lay flat on the grass looking at the stars in the sky, while Flick and I sat up mesmerized by the twinkling skyline, talking about anything and everything that came to mind. Oh, what a life!

34

Rotto

I didn't realize that going to Rottnest was going to be such an event. I imagined a calm, relaxing ferry taking us to an island where there would be serviced beds by the ocean. Flick purchased the early morning tickets and we had to be up at five am and to the ferry for six am. I also didn't realize the ferry was an express, that bounced chaotically across the waves causing me to feel quite sick. When we got to the island, Flick took us to our bikes and asked which way we wanted to cycle.

"We cycle, all day?" I asked her, confused.

"Yes, I mean there is a bus, but I prefer cycling around, then you don't have to wait and you can leave whenever you want," Sel and I looked at each other, not prepared physically or mentally for cycling all day. We decided to cycle toward the left of the island first, because she recommended Salmon Bay, saying it was the prettiest. It was. The glistening flat turquoise waters, with yachts on the horizon. There were people lying in the sun, some under umbrellas and some trying to find shade under their shirts. There were people with snorkels, far into the distance and water so clear I could see the vast amount of coral reef beneath the surface. The water was freezing, but felt therapeutic after the initial breathtaking icy sting. We stayed for about thirty minutes and Flick wanted to take us to the next spot. I went to cycle left again, following the path we came, but she started cycling in the opposite direction.

"Nope, this way, I just wanted to take you here first because I always come here last and never have enough time for it or am too exhausted for it." And so we went back in the direction we came, passing the tourist information centre and the jetty.

"OMG, what's that little furry thing?" Sel yelled out, pointing to a small possum-looking animal.

"It's a quokka, they are famous to Rotto, one of the only places they are found in the world." She stopped her bike but didn't get off. Sel and I did though, intrigued. We didn't want to be a tourist that overwhelmed the poor creature, but to be fair, it did look like it was having the time of its life, while tourists were taking selfies with it.

"Can we?" I asked Flick, who put her bike to the side and came to join us. At first, she was angling her phone taking a photo for us, and then she switched it to selfie mode. All three of us smiling at the camera, Flick's arm stretching as far as she could go to get the famous #quokka-selfie as it was nibbling on grass, not concerned as to what antics we were doing around it. Then we continued the cycle, stopping at various different beaches until we were ready to hop on our bikes and explore another one. There were twists and turns, and hills, so many hills, that Sel and I both had to get off our bikes and walk them up multiple times. The sun was hot, my thighs were burning and it was the biggest relief when Flick said it was finally time to turn around and head to the pub for an ice-cold beer, sharing tables and accomplished, exhausted looks with everyone else who had endured the same beautiful pain we had.

"What are your thoughts on the next couple of days now?" Flick said, an ice-cold Matso's ginger beer with lime squeezed in it half empty in front of her, all of us drinking it so quickly the ice cubes we requested they add barely melted inside the glass.

"To be honest, something a little more relaxing than this please," I responded with laughter, Sel nodding in agreeance, her beer against her lips taking another sip.

"Well, we know we love this ginger beer by the beach, let's try the wine in the south?" Sel said.

"Done. We can have a sleep in tomorrow, and maybe head down after lunch? That will give me a bit of time in the morning to get some work done?" Flick said matter-of-factly, looking up toward the sky like she was putting a plan together in her mind. We began googling different places to go, and looking if there were any winery charters available at such short notice. We kept going like this until we noticed people had started getting up and heading back to the ferry. We looked at the time and did the same, finding our bikes and this time walking them over, knowing the bike seat imprint was going to be sore if we tried to get on it again.

We looked back onto the island as the ferry started speeding away, the glistening turquoise blue waters against the soft white sand, slowly disappearing into the distance, a core memory of the most beautiful island I have ever been to implanting itself in my memory. This is exactly what I thought Australia was going to be about.

35

Douth

"I thought you said we could sleep in?" Sel said to Flick, as she was opening the blinds in the lounge room and putting her kettle on. She always had a warm lemon water in the morning, a ritual that we took part in while we were with her because it screamed #health although we didn't know why. Flick decided it would be great to have breakfast by the coast, in Cottesloe, so we could get a beach dip in and mark it off our bucket list.

"I'm getting through your wish list as much as possible, I don't know how much colder it will feel down south and you may not get a chance again. We will have breakfast and a dip in Cottesloe, it's one of the top beaches here and then stop into Freo, sorry … I mean, Fremantle … for some treats or lunch before heading down south," she said. We agreed with her and started getting ready.

The temperature heated quickly in the morning and by nine am it was maybe eighty degrees Fahrenheit. The air was still and water was flat in Cottesloe, though I still found it ice cold. Flick and Sel dove in, I struggled, slowly moving in bit by bit until it hit my waist, and then decided I better look after our belongings on the sand.

"I better not get my hair wet, I'll take too long to get ready," I lied, truly feeling like the water was so cold it was burning with each step, making my heart race. We dried off, had breakfast, and made our way back to the apartment to pack for Margaret River, managing to book everything the night before.

We stopped into Fremantle, which took about thirty minutes to get to. At first Flick drove around to point out some sites like the Fremantle Prison, explaining how it was a UNESCO World Heritage site and how they did underground tunnel tours. I admired the Victorian-era architecture and hidden street art, taking pictures as we strolled through the streets with our coffees to the Fremantle Markets. We picked up snacks for the ride – chocolate, donuts – and Sel and I picked up a few souvenirs as well. A fridge magnet here, a diary there.

After a two-hour drive south, our next stop was the Bunbury Farmers Market; the prettiest grocery store I have ever experienced. It was like a food version of Ikea; one-way zone, full of fresh colorful local produce. We picked up healthier food options here – salads and soups – to last us for the next couple of days and tried our first meat pies and sausage rolls with ketchup, confused at first when she asked me if I wanted 'tomato sauce'. Full to the brim, we continued our drive for another hour or so, through flat terrain passing paddocks of cows and sheep. As we reached closer, tall trees lined the winding roads and it reminded me of the drive to Mom's house. We got to our accommodation in Margaret River, a cosy self-contained house, surrounded by bushland, the smell of eucalyptus wafting through the air. We parked in the carport and found the lockbox with the key and made our way inside, leaving our bags in the car so we could scope the place out. The ceiling was high, with the entry hall splitting into left and right. The left had the bedrooms and bathrooms, while the right turn led us to the kitchen and lounge area; a completely open-plan living area with large windows that opened the space and made it feel very elegant. There was a black fireplace against the left wall, and a white ten-seater couch surrounding it, with a heavy jarrah wood coffee table between. There was an eight-seater dining table, with a large abstract painting hanging on the wall next to it. The kitchen had an island in the middle, with stainless steel appliances throughout, everything neatly in its place and a binder on the island.

"This place is stunning," I said, walking around, noticing all the high-end finishings. I heard Flick open the fridge and the kitchen cupboards, the sound of each one closing causing an echo.

"Surely this is someone's holiday home, there are hundreds of different teas and spices here, the cabinets are full." It was about four pm and we were all tired from the big day, so we brought our bags in, moved into the rooms we wanted and then congregated back in the kitchen, opening a glass of red wine and putting the TV on for background noise. Sel put the oven on and unboxed one of the pizzas and salads we had bought in Bunbury, while I started looking at different board games I found stacked on the TV cabinet that we could potentially play.

"So, we have a half past ten pickup, who's keen for a walk in the morning?" Flick asked us, knowing we would do it if she was.

"Then first stop, we are going to Walsh & Son, lunch at Xanadu, tastings at Lenton Brae and then beer at Beerfarm. Then back home for pizzas and snacks?" I read out the notes on my phone slowly, not sure if I was pronouncing anything right.

"You got it, gf," said Flick cheerily, "I might actually go to bed early then, big day tomorrow. Walk at eight am?" We nodded, she threw back the last of the wine and put her glass in the sink, "Night, see you both tomorrow." Sel and I put on a movie. Sel finished watching it, but I hung up my boots and called it a night too, making sure to message Gary and send him a few pictures before falling asleep.

36

Wine

We were woken by birds chirping. I could hear kookaburras laughing, and a plethora of other birds too. There were roosters in the distance and the sun was beaming through the windows. I could hear the sound of the kettle about to boil, indicating that Flick was up making her warm lemon water, and I heard someone in the shower – must be Sel. I checked my phone and slowly made my way to the kitchen, hair a mess in oversized pyjamas. Flick had three mugs in front of her, already in her workout gear.

"Do you think staying fit helps with travelling?" I asked her, thinking about how she had travelled so much of the world herself, and how that must require a lot of energy, mentally and physically, but also confidence.

"I would say it probably helps with recovering, but I guess I don't feel I'm on holiday while I'm in my home state. I don't make warm lemon water travelling, and I usually don't get up to exercise because there is so much walking all day to be honest," she said, and she made a point. If I was back home, I would probably also be in the routine of walks, or yoga or Pilates. They were my forms of exercise, although I had always been inconsistent with it. I changed into workout clothes, and when the three of us finished drinking our warm lemon water, we all went for a walk to explore the bushland area we were staying in. We started to stroll along the grey asphalt road filled with holes, which we had to walk along as the red gravel seemed slippery. The area was hilly, and a part of me was worried a coyote might jump out, however Flick assured me there were none in Western Australia. The air was cooler than in the city, and the roads were empty, with no cars passing us as we followed its curve in different directions, until there was an open field. Sel and I didn't know where we were, allowing Flick to take the lead.

"Look," she said, suddenly stopping, as two kangaroos were eating grass on the opposite side of the road. They were so close, their heads pricking up as they watched us stand still and after a moment, went back to eating. I took out my phone quickly, and the sudden movement made them jump away, videoing as much as I could in those moments.

"They are literally like jumping deer, it's actually weird," Sel said, still staring in the direction they went. I thought about the last time I had seen a big animal. Living in Manhattan and then moving to Hawaii, I realized there were very little animals I had seen. I didn't see many in London, Iceland, Scotland, India, in fact, I couldn't remember seeing very many in Mexico when I was there with Mark either.

"I think this is the most wildlife I've seen in years," I said curiously, not sure if it was true or if I hadn't remembered. *Maybe on the way to Mom's house I might have seen deer when I was visiting her?*

"I must say, we are very lucky here in WA, in Australia really, we have such a thriving ecosystem. We are really lucky." I could see her face change, a sense of pride maybe, but clearly pondering how grateful she was.

When we got back to the house, we took turns showering and getting ready; two people in the kitchen making breakfast while the third showered, and then it swapped, until we were all fed, showered and ready to go. The group bus came at ten-thirty am on the dot to start the wine tour, and there were four other groups already onboard. There were two couples, an older husband and wife and mother and daughter. The bus was quiet to start, with the operator introducing each person as they came onboard. We were the last pickup, and we went straight to the first venue – Walsh & Son. Everyone quietly sat, as the tasters were being poured, discussing politely the notes and if they liked it after each sip. The second stop at Xanadu for lunch involved us leaving the table for taste testers and buying a bottle each, and then joining the table with another glass of wine, increasing the mingling. By Lenton Brae, the three of us had split up, taking turns talking to everyone else, the alcohol creating more comfort as we went on. By Beerfarm, no-one was solely talking to the person they were on the bus with. We had all formed various bonds, talking together at a big table, beer paddles now in front of us, exchanging numbers and social media, if they had it.

"Why is it that everyone on the bus was Australian do you think?" Sel asked Flick.

"I think we just like to get drunk and make a day out of it, but also because of the lack of transport it's easier to do a public tour bus."

It made sense to me. It was like how the girls and I would go to Niagara Falls for the wine tours, or Napa Valley. It's mostly to have a big day out of it. I didn't know if I would do it as I got older if I was travelling to another country.

"Anyone want to continue on at the pub?" Flick asked the group. All, except the older couple, said *yes*. The bus driver dropped us at the pub with our bottles of wine and we continued into the night, eyeing off groups of guys and chatting the night away with the other two couples that joined us too. I wondered if we would ever see the bottles of wine we bought again, thinking back to wine tours I had done with my friends back home, how we had drunkenly left them somewhere during the night.

37

Dylan

We managed to stumble our way back to our Airbnb, a few guys in tow, where we played games we had out from the night before. All three of us managing to connect with a cute Australian guy, ticking off another checklist for Sel. They were visiting for a friend's bucks' the next day, and didn't plan on such a big night, however we stayed up until two am playing charades until Flick called it first to go to bed; all the bottles we purchased sitting empty on the kitchen island.

We woke up to the sound of the boys making us – or them – breakfast, pots and pans clanking together and the smell of bacon wafting through the house. I walked out to the table neatly set with six plates on it and coffees being made. There was a plate with bread smothered in black salty paste that I learned was 'Vegemite' that they prepared for Sel and I to try. I didn't like it, but the gesture was sweet.

"This is what Australian guys are like?" I asked, bewildered and wondering if I should move to Australia instead. We were sitting on the couch as they handed us freshly made coffees.

"Ahh, not that I've experienced if I'm being honest. I would say that maybe yes, but they would also still ask you to split dinner fifty-fifty," Flick said chuckling, although I couldn't tell if she had laced it with sarcasm.

"Feminism, it's not our fault," Rory yelled from the kitchen, pan in his hand, serving the scrambled eggs. Flick rolled her eyes, clearly acknowledging she knew where this conversation was going to lead. They piled out after we'd eaten, exchanging numbers and calling a taxi, while we began to clean up.

"You guys should join us later tonight. We'll be back there with all the boys … we could do this again."

"We'll think about it," Sel said, kissing Alex on the cheek and pushing him toward the door, now ushering for everyone to leave. As soon as they did, Sel and Flick turned to me. I don't think the front door had even shut behind the guys yet.

"What about Gary?" they said in tune, high-pitched with widened cheeky eyes.

"I know, I know. Dylan kissed me and I kissed him back, that's it. We had so much to drink yesterday, and it happened so naturally. I figured Gary and I aren't official official as well. Who knows what he's wrapping up at home as well, you know?" I said, accentuating the second 'official' when I spoke and not making eye contact with them, reflecting the guilt I felt. I was pushing the food scraps into the bin, one plate at a time. Gary and I had spoken every few days on the trip, but we both knew we were taking it slow. *What's the harm in a little drunken Australian kiss?*

"Should we stay another night?" Flick asked, all of us a little googly-eyed after such a fun evening. "It's up to you guys, you leave tomorrow. What else did you want to do?" Sel and I looked at our notes.

"Anything we should do?"

"I mean, we've ticked off the easiest things on your list. We could drive up to the Pinnacles if you wanted, they are termite mounds. There are tonnes of beaches and places to eat in and around Perth — but there is also plenty to see around here. We could look at some of the caves. There's a lighthouse where the Southern and Indian oceans meet."

"I'm digging Alex, if I'm being honest," Sel piped up. "It's been a long time since I've had that kind of chemistry with someone." Flick agreed, telling us all the details about her and Rory.

"Not that I want to stay for boys, but it sounds like there is still so much to see here. So, two birds, one stone? We stay," I said, as Flick logged online to check if we could stay another night. We could, and then we planned how we wanted to explore the rest of the day, and telling the guys we would meet them later that night for the fun to continue. Flick drove us to the beaches, the lighthouse and to her favorite cave – Ngilgi cave – where we put on a hard hat and lamp, venturing off the boardwalk and learning about Aboriginal history behind the land on a self-guided tour.

When the evening came, I watched how Flick cosied up to Alex again, and how Sel went straight to the dance floor with Rory. I wished Gary was there.

"You're dating someone, hey?" Dylan asked, putting two beers down in front of us, taking a seat next to me. I nodded.

"I mean, it's not official, but we have a thing, and I don't want to do wrong by him."

"It's cool. We don't need to do anything, last night was fun. And must have been meant to happen, cause look at these guys. Who would have thought … on a bucks'?" he chuckled to himself.

We talked about how he worked fly-in fly-out to the mines, many of the guys did, so had a full week off work. He shared how difficult it was for them to be away from family and friends, especially to attempt dating, but they enjoyed the lifestyle and the money. He quickly threw in he had recently gotten divorced as well.

"She just couldn't deal with me being away anymore, which I get, but I didn't want to go back to working five days a week either. Gosh, only getting two days a week off, I can't imagine anymore," he said. I could understand that. It was the same kind of feeling I had when I thought about working a corporate job again. I don't know if I could do it, for anyone. His hazel eyes, staring deeply into mine as we shared intimate things about ourselves. I could feel a connection forming.

"Are you dating?" I asked him. "You're a good-looking guy."

He blushed. "I tried the online app thing, but it's not for me. I'll meet someone when I'm supposed to," he shrugged, nonchalantly, potentially hiding his true feelings. I didn't know. But we sat there, watching everyone around us, enjoying each other's company without any other expectations, only Flick and Sel giving me the occasional cheeky side-eye. A warmth engulfed my body once more, in awe of where another spontaneous decision had led us. *Could life always be this simple and beautiful if we just let it?*

38

Next

We ended up driving back to Perth with the boys, spending our last evening with them in the city before we said our goodbyes and goodnights, with Flick finally taking us to the airport. I wished it could have been a more intimate goodbye with Flick and Sel, but I knew they were both free spirits, it's what I adored about them both – their spontaneity and how open they are to new connections – and I knew they wouldn't have entertained these guys if there wasn't a genuine connection.

"Well, that was unexpected," I said to them in the car, a sadness coming over me at the thought of leaving Flick, never being good at the goodbyes.

"Isn't it all," Flick said driving, her eyes twinkling as she drove. Sel had the same look, both of their cheeks rosier than usual. They told me about their spicy stories, and I told them how Dylan and I just played board games and drank beers. It was enough for me. I didn't need anything more and I was glad he was respectful.

"Think you'll see Rory again?" I asked Sel. She nodded, her grin wide. It reminded me of when I first met Gary, the chemistry, the excitement, but also the unknown. *Will we see them again? Or was it a fleeting moment we will only talk about again when the three of us are together – if we ever are?* The highs of travel, so perfectly and almost tragically woven with the sadness of it. The sadness of hugging them at the airport and never knowing when you will see them again.

"Honestly, that was such a ride, thank you so much, Flick," I said, hugging her, her curly hair tickling my nose but savoring the moment, that warm hug she gives, one that goes on for a second longer than you want it to, but it's really the amount of time we need. We left Flick at the security gate, watching each other while we lined up and went through, then made our way to the departure gate.

Flying into Sydney at night was mesmerizing, peering out of the window, grateful for yet another window seat.

"Is that the harbor bridge?" I asked, as we were descending. Sel leaning over toward me to try and get a glimpse. The city lights glistening beneath us, from what looked like glitter slowly getting larger to make out street lights and car headlights moving through the streets. The city looked bustling, much bigger than Perth.

We got our bags and headed to the taxi rank, Sel looking for places open around us.

"Want to go to the Opera Bar when we land?" she asked. I was ready to go to sleep at this point. We had five days here and didn't feel the need to explore.

"You go, I might have a quiet one tonight," I suggested. She hesitated at first, unsure if she needed to do the same, or maybe she was testing her own confidence levels.

"Okay, sure, that will be good for me too I think," she said. We definitely recharged in our own ways. While Sel liked time to herself, it was still generally doing something like a walk or a drink. When I needed to recharge, I wanted silence and to be alone with as little stimulation as possible.

"Want me to take your bags up?" I asked her. "If you're anything like me, once you sit down up there you might not leave again tonight." She took up the offer, wheeling her suitcase close to me, loaded a map on her mobile and strolled out, asking if I wanted any food or drinks on her way back, to which I declined, already planning to order room service and eat it in the bath, alone.

The room had two queen beds overlooking the bridge and Opera House, the calm water reflecting the lights on the shore, everything glistening. I looked at the checklist of what Sel and I had planned on the flight; bridge climb, Opera House cruise, zoo. I took this time to check in with Gary, who was selling furniture, slowly clearing out his belongings and one step closer to the big New York move. I considered telling him about the kiss with Dylan, but didn't want to complicate things unnecessarily. Then I spent time scrolling through social media looking through Flick and Sel's update, checking Dylan's stories, liking the pictures finally being posted from Ads' engagement party. And when I felt my checklist had been completed, I ordered a steak, potatoes and red wine to the room and turned on the bath, squeezing in the shower gel the hotel provided. Five more days left until back to Hawaii, and then starting my life again in Manhattan. *What does Sydney have in store for us?*

39

Sydney

I must have fallen asleep before Sel got home, as it was pitch black when I woke up. Sel had closed the sunshades, as the city lights were too bright for her. I flicked one of the multiple switches by my bedside table, hoping it was for the lamp on my side, accidentally turning all the lights on in the entire room. I quickly flicked them back off at the same time as Sel groaned.

"Sorry," I whispered, now opting for my phone torch, which felt the safer bet, making my way quietly to the bathroom. I started getting ready so I'd be in time for breakfast, and after I'd showered and washed my face, I put my phone torch back on. But as I opened the bathroom door, Sydney was already bustling in front of us.

"Wow, what a view," Sel said, standing in her pyjamas by the full length windows. It was even better seeing it during the day, watching the boats cruise around, and the vast water stretching through the city. She yawned, coupled with a stretch, and went to her suitcase to take her own to shower. We had both learned about each other's schedules. I always woke up the first to shower, and generally, by the time I had finished, Sel would be up and get ready. She used me as an alarm clock, but I liked it, as it allowed me to set the pace for the day.

"Are you happy to stroll today?" I asked her, my voice louder to make sure she heard me in the bathroom.

"Want to do the zoo? I hear it's a good one here," she yelled back, the shower streaming in the background.

"Yup," I said, lying back on my bed and looking at my phone, trying to gage distances and public transport.

We walked through the streets, as Sel had done last night, caught trains and buses wherever we needed to, without any rush or time frame. Our time in Perth almost gave us the permission to slow down, even though the city was bustling and moving faster around us. After Taronga Zoo, we strolled passed a tattoo parlour that I didn't notice, but Sel did.

"Katie," she paused, her eyes darting, "can we?" I watched as her eyes lit up looking at the tattoo parlour. *This was so Sel.*

"A tattoo? What? No!" I exclaimed, as she grabbed my hand and dragged me inside. I was immediately nervous, my virgin skin standing out amongst many whose skins were filled in.

"What a way to remember this trip of ours," she said, and I couldn't *not* agree. She was right. It would be a trip forever etched within me. Sel booked for both of us, flicking through pages of flash options they had.

"What would we get?" I asked, thinking of different ways to summarize India and Australia.

"A wine glass, a lotus?" she asked. I pondered.

"What about … a bee, my Bumble BFF?" we both looked at each other smiling, realizing it wasn't the places we wanted to remember, but the memories together of us.

An hour later, we finished our stroll, taking a seat at the nearest bar with panoramic views of the bridge and the Opera House, images of bees firmly covered with plastic on our inner elbows, and smiles spread across our faces.

Sel hovered her phone over the QR code. "A bottle?" she confirmed, without really needing to. I nodded with a look of approval. We knew this was it for us for the day, enjoying each other's company and watching the day pass us by. She was on her phone a bit more than usual too, sending pictures of her new tattoo to someone.

"Alex?" I asked, as a cheeky smile spread across her face.

"He is going to visit me in Hawaii. We had a real connection, Katie," she said, taking another sip of the sparkling. I was watching the bubbles rise from the bottom of the glass to pop at the top. She told me she had once considered moving to Australia too, but it had always seemed so far, so out of the way, so out of her sight. But here she was now, experiencing both sides of the country and then meeting someone so unexpectedly. *What are the chances?*

As the sun slowly set and the skies changed, food was coming and going from our table, with another bottle, and then we strolled back to our hotel. The rest of our time in Sydney felt like this, like a relaxing experience with only one event a day. Our second day we went shopping and strolled around the Queen Victoria Building, looking at unique fashion and buying organic this and chocolate that, spending our evening enjoying our first opera, not realizing the profound effect it would have on me, a surprising tear rolling down my cheek at the end. Our third day, we woke up early to climb the Sydney Harbour Bridge and then ventured to Bondi Beach, although it didn't compare to the Perth beaches, it was too busy. On the fourth day we went to Manly Beach and continued to eat our way through the city, trying anything we hadn't yet; roasted lamb, lamingtons, pavlova. Although a little hard to find, the local supermarkets, Coles or Woolworths, always came to our rescue.

It had been nearly six weeks of travelling and fatigue was setting in. The initial energy we had meeting new people and exploring was growing tired. We were losing patience with crowds, lines and dining out, craving being alone more than usual and a simple, home-cooked meal.

"Did that go quick or slow for you?" I asked Sel, as we were both packing our bags for the final time of the trip, ready to venture back home, both feeling it was time to start the next phase of our lives.

"Both; it started slow, then it went quick, then slow and now I can't believe it's already over." I agreed with her. There was something surreal about knowing we had travelled across three continents, experienced different cultures and had the flexibility to push our trip out to *Australia*.

40

Mark

It was a feeling of safety, of calmness, when I finally dropped my bags in the lounge room of John's home, thankful to be in his presence again. He had picked us both up from the airport and dropped Sel home on the way. His nature being genuinely inquisitive, he asked me lots of questions, and not only the surface-level ones of *what did you see?* and *where did you go?* but things like *how did you feel in the waters of Kerala?* And *what lessons did you learn?* It made me reflect on my time once again. From the kind nature of all the people we met in India, how lucky I was to live and be able to afford to continue to live in western culture, how my business had thrived and the fact I was in Hawaii in the first place with Mark, which gave me the opportunity to stay there for the last twelve months. I had an overwhelming feeling of gratitude that I had bumped into Flick, and it gave me faith that everything all works out, Whether it is all a coincidence or whether it's divine timing. I thought about the synchronicities of meeting Flick, how that took us to Australia, how her and Sel met those guys down south. *Who knows how these interactions will continue to shape us?*

The trip felt like a reset. It gave me perspective I needed again, and it made me excited for what was to come, packing up and leaving Hawaii again, seeing Sel flourish working for the art gallery, seeing my family again and starting my business in New York. I was excited to get some pictures from the trip onto the walls in the gallery before I left too. I was excited to see Gary again and see how his new business venture goes, to spend time showing him around Brooklyn, where I grew up, and also discover it again for myself.

It was a rush of excitement that fuelled me as I navigated the final photoshoots before leaving. I was focused and driven, fuelled by purpose.

I was at a photoshoot for a new Hawaiian surf wear brand, when a text message took me by surprise.

Hi Katie, would you be open to having a chat? Mark

My tummy turned, instantly and instinctively when seeing his name. I wasn't sure if it was acid rising in my gut, grateful I was working so I could distract myself, my mind aggressively pushing questions into it, so that even when I was focusing on work, there was this transparent overlay of – *why is Mark wanting to talk?*

When the shoot was over, three hours later, I responded: Sure what's up. The curiosity getting the better of me.

Mark: Can I call you?

Me: Now? I'll be home in an hour, but sure.

I wrapped up what I needed to in the studio I hired, and the entire time I was travelling back home, my mind was racing. *Was it Luna? Is someone sick? Is he … dying?* Luckily, the hour flew by. And as the last few seconds clocked over to three pm, the phone rang, and the acidic feeling in my stomach, this time, shocked my entire body.

"Mark? Is everything okay?" I asked, genuinely concerned he would only have bad news for me.

"Everything is fine, Katie, how are you?" he asked. He sounded fine, his voice slow and paced, slightly deeper than I remember it, but I'd known him for long enough to know he wanted to tell me something he felt unsure about telling me. He always spoke like that when he wanted to keep me calm.

"I'm good, got back from India and Australia a couple of weeks ago, so catching up on work and then wrapping things up before moving back to New York," I told him, not remembering if I had shared that much with him in a long time.

"Wow, that sounds amazing. Sounds like you had a great time," he responded, the line then went silent. I was waiting for him to say something, but he didn't.

"Hello? Are you there?" He muttered a *yes*, and then it went silent again. "What's going on, Mark, what do you need to tell me?" I pressed, getting frustrated and worried.

"I miss you, Katie." *Miss me? He called to tell me he misses me? This time.* I went silent. "Would you be open to catching up for a coffee, to chat about us when you're back?" he added. I was stunned. I never thought he would call me like this, someone who was filled with ego and pride.

"Oh. I wasn't expecting that. Are you … okay Mark? Is everything alright?" I said again, leaving spaces in my words but naturally accentuating okay and alright.

"I'm fine. I've just realized how much I miss you, and it would be good to catch up to talk if you're open to it." *Was I open to it?* I wasn't sure. I hadn't thought about it. I felt I'd moved on with my life. It had been over a year now.

"I mean, we can catch up when I'm back if you like, in a month or so but I don't know what to say. I didn't think I would see you again, if I'm being honest." I wanted to be honest. I didn't know if there was any point, but after eight years, I was fine to give him a conversation if he needed it. He told me how he started seeing a psychologist and realized how much of his life he was giving to work without getting anything in return. His life had felt empty and while being partner was his focus before, he'd realized there is so much more to life. *Was it too late?*

41

Move

I finished finalizing the procedures for Sel and John, making sure I had access to all my prints online and gave Sel an induction, with John there too, so he knew the changes I made when he was away to make the business more efficient. He already knew from looking after the place for the six weeks I was away, but I wanted to reiterate it, as I knew he would also likely cut corners without me.

"You've done such a great job, Katie. You've bettered my business, you've introduced me to, Sel. You're really making our worlds an easier place, thank you." I could feel my heart warm, and the sting of tears being held back.

"You're going to make me cry, John, stop," I said, as he came in to hug me and I allowed two tears to stream down my face.

"This isn't a goodbye. You have shoots you have to be back for, so I'll see you then and you can always stay at my place, no questions asked. My home is always going to be your home."

"Going to miss you, babe," said Sel, as she came in to hug me too. I could feel my flight time slowly drawing nearer, the day somehow flying by with a small regret of not booking a later flight. My bags were packed, and I had sent two parcels to Aunty Rita in Brooklyn, the neighbor we grew up with. Mom said she would pick me up from the airport and take me to Brooklyn when I got in. I hadn't told her in the rush of travelling and wrapping up most of my life in Hawaii that Gary was going to be living at the house too. I didn't think she would care but I knew I had to tell her. I probably needed to tell someone about Mark too, but I wanted to keep some things for me, so I could know how I felt about it before allowing others' opinions and limiting beliefs to impact me, surely it did subconsciously. It had to.

I told Sel and John I didn't want them to come into the airport with me. I wanted time alone and I didn't want to make the departure sadder than I already felt, so we said goodbye at the drop-off point, tears running down my face as soon as I turned to walk away from them, toward the airport doors. Wiping my tears, I looked back with blurred vision, both of them still standing outside of the car making sure I safely made it inside, John's arm around Sel's shoulders, Sel wiping tears away too. I took a deep inhale, and a longer exhale.

Waiting for my flight, I took out my phone to make plans.

Settle > Sort finance > Business plan > Gary

First, I wanted to make sure the house was comfortable again. It still had boxes and old furniture from when I grew up. The house was essentially a storage unit in suburbia. Mom agreed I could stay for as long as I needed and pay her a small amount of rent and the bills. However, I could spend my own money fixing it up in any way I wanted to. I wanted to repaint, give it a refresh and make it feel like home.

Next, I needed to figure out where I was financially. *What were my financial goals? How much money did I have to live on without any income?* Which led me naturally to my business plan.

Did I want to continue with weddings and branding? Did I want to expand into travel, journalism even? How much money did I want to earn? What did I want my life to look like?

Then there was Gary. *What were we? Were we compatible?* I wanted to make sure I wasn't living my life blindly, like I did with Mark. It took me eight years to realize I was walking through life like a robot, not experiencing anything new or doing the things I wanted to do. I knew that wasn't me anymore, but it did make me nervous that I could easily fall into the same trap. *What did I want a relationship to look like? Was it something he was ready for and something we needed to talk about before he moved in? When he moved in?*

Gary and I were consistently talking again once I arrived back in Hawaii. He was very close to being ready to leave Scotland, in fact, just two weeks away. I had sent him pictures of what the property looked like and explained what I wanted to do with it. We were going to split the low rent, so he felt he was chipping in as well.

"What if things don't work out though? Will you be upset you put extra money in?"

"What? Of course not, Katie. You are still doing me a favor, and what if it does work out?" he said, his deep voice so calm, soft and sure. I knew it was a good a time as any to bring up my concerns.

"Do you think it's all too much too soon? I'm of course happy to have you stay, but what are we? Friends living together? Are we dating? What do you want?" I asked, not truly sure what I wanted.

"It's hard to say when we've hardly spent any real time together. We definitely haven't been dating because I haven't taken you on a date," he laughed, bringing lightness to the conversation.

"I'm asking, because … well, I need you to know I kissed someone in Australia, and I've been feeling so guilty about it," I finally said, my shoulders dropping in relief. There was silence.

"It's okay, Katie. We never talked about it before I left. We should have, but there was so much going on," he said calmy.

"And … well … Mark called and wanted to catch up," I said, this time my voice talking slow and calm, choosing my words carefully.

"For what?" he answered quickly this time, his voice still not changing.

You could cut the tension through the phone this time.

"To talk about us. I said I would, but I thought I should tell you. I get that we can't label anything, but I said I would go and hear him out."

"I understand, do you … still think about him?" he asked, his voice straining slightly now.

"Not at all, it completely took me by surprise. I thought something had happened to Luna," I responded. I reassured Gary it was nothing and hoped it had also planted a seed of considering what we are before he got to Brooklyn. We agreed we would stay in separate rooms while we figured things out, to take the pressure off. I had discovered that Gary had also never lived with a woman before. There were girlfriends here and there, but never a long-term relationship.

"I just never met someone I wanted to commit to like that, I guess," he said when I asked him about it. I didn't know how he would go with my hair falling around the place, and my skin products cluttering the bathroom, or even how we would feel sharing one toilet.

When the flight landed in New York, the first face I saw was Mom's, in my favorite big red jacket of hers and clutching onto her extra-large handbag that had water and snacks in it for the drive home. It was on the drive home I filled her in about Gary.

"Oh, that spunk in the picture you showed me," she said, cheekily, reminding me of the way she would talk to me in middle school when she saw me talking to a boy. "I can leave my car with you if you like? For him to use. You can drop me home tomorrow." I adored the relationship we had built together, she had never been anything more than kind and helpful to me during this time, especially through the break up and the move, always knowing when to give me love and when to give me space.

When we got to the property in Brooklyn, I saw the packages sent from Hawaii in the lounge room. She had a bottle of red wine on the kitchen counter with two glasses next to my favorite snacks, and then I saw *her* running toward me.

"Luna!" I dropped to my knees as she jumped into my arms, her excitement quivering through her tiny body telling me she missed me too. I sat on the couch with her in my lap as Mom handed me a glass of wine and put the bottle on the table between us. "Oh … and Mark wants to catch up and talk about us," I threw in, surprising us both. She didn't need to say a thing, the look in her eyes said it all.

42

Brooklyn

"I can't believe you're here," I said excitedly, throwing my arms around him as he walked through the arrivals gate. It had been months since I'd seen him in Hawaii and felt a mix of excitement and nerves about seeing him again. We settled for a kiss on the cheek, his brown bristly beard tickling my skin, before he enveloped me in a long, comforting hug. He had just flown in from Edinburgh and he was wheeling two very large suitcases on a trolley, I teased, "Surely that's over thirty pounds?"

"Something like that. I cleared as much as I could, gave the rest to Mom for storage and I felt like I needed all of this. One is winter and one is summer, essentially."

"Do you need anything? Otherwise, let's go … home," I asked awkwardly. We both looked at each other and laughed. I had missed laughing with him, his laugh resonated from deep in his chest. "Mom left her car with me, so you can use it for as long as you need. We are pretty good with public transport here, but see how you go and we can drop it off to her if we find we don't need it. Is that okay?"

"Of course it is. Thanks so much. I really appreciate all of this." I couldn't stop admiring him, his rugged charm and Scottish accent.

As we made our way home, he talked about how it was leaving the pub in Edinburgh, how they had a goodbye party and all the regulars came in, including Alice and Uncle Pat. They had his farewell in the local newspaper and posted it all over social media. It turned out to be their biggest night of the year, it exceeded Christmas. It was wild how humble Gary was, like he didn't know why so many people would turn up for his farewell. I don't think he realized the inclusive environment he made for people in his community and how empty the place would feel without him.

"How did your Mom go? I know you two are close," I asked.

"It was hard, she cried, I tried my best not to cry. The guys at the pub down the road check in on her and will look after her. I told her I would check with you but would you be okay with her visiting whenever she wanted?" he said.

"Yes, of course. You will need to sleep in the lounge when she does though. We have four bedrooms, but I figured we would both need a working space." He smirked, but knew he was thinking about whether or not we would be sharing a bed. I had spent a good two weeks by myself, making our old family home a little bit more modern. Reluctantly, Mom let me give away some of the furniture and clear out old things that had been sitting there since we were kids and didn't need anymore. While she was happy for me to repaint, it turned out she wasn't so happy with me disposing of sentimental things.

"It's about time," both my siblings said when we discussed it as a family. Mom was a bit of a hoarder. I think she was worried she would forget. I spent a few days seeing friends, my brother and sister and their families. I did a post-wedding shoot for Adeline in the city to make up for not taking pictures at her engagement (turned wedding), which doubled to use in my New York portfolio to create traction for local enquiries. I could see my new life coming together. So, when Gary arrived, I was more than ready for his company.

"I guess I'll take this room," Gary said as he looked around the house, walking down the small hallway and putting his bags in the empty room. There weren't too many places to go and he had finished in about a minute. Enough time for me to unbox the takeaway containers and open a beer for him and pour a red wine for myself. He took a shower, and came out dressed in fresh casual clothes, a white cotton tee and black slacks, much to my disappointment when I had hoped for just a towel.

"I know this place is small but hopefully it will do for now," I said, as he walked up to me. My heart fluttered and a tingle cascaded throughout my entire body. He kissed me, first lightly on the lips and then his tongue enveloped mine, filling my mouth. It was calming, soothing, soft. Not exhilarating like I had imagined, like Hawaii was, but maybe that was because of the secrecy around my family. I liked this.

"I've been wanting to do that since the airport, but I wanted you to feel comfortable," he said. Even that care made my legs quiver. I felt awkward, shy maybe.

"Are you hungry?" I changed the subject, not because I didn't want to savor the moment, but because I didn't want to rush and risk something going wrong too soon. He nodded as I gestured toward the dining table, placing our plates on it, and sitting opposite him, taking a sip of wine first. We updated each other on all that had been happening, all the problems with the restaurant and I told him about how my business had slowly been growing too.

"So, did you ever meet up with Mark?" he asked, when the conversation relaxed. I hadn't told anyone I had yet.

"I did. We caught up and he told me how sorry he was, but I told him about you moving here and that I was really happy. He didn't seem surprised that we reconnected after, but he didn't make any smart or mean comments about it, which made me feel he had grown. Too much time had passed, there wasn't all that much we talked about to be honest. I want to move forward."

"Why did you entertain it?" he asked inquisitively, I could feel the jealousy in his voice, or maybe it was genuine confusion or curiosity, but I appreciated the direct eye contact he was giving me. I missed looking into those deep brown eyes. Mark always avoiding my gaze during our conversation.

"I just think, because it was eight years, it's a long time. No-one cheated or did anything bad. I was happy to give him space to talk out of respect and kindness but he's in the past now," I said. I felt confident about why I did it, even if Gary didn't agree. He pondered it for a moment, and I noticed he let out a deep sigh, seeming to have let it go. He nodded, and I was grateful to leave Mark in the past.

43

Beginnings

When I woke in my bed the next morning, it was no surprise that Gary was still lying there. This was the first morning we had the luxury of it. When we were in Hawaii, I was getting up before him to leave, or ducking off to go home late at night so the family wouldn't see me. As I stirred, he pulled me closer, my body fitting perfectly against his. He moved my long dark brown hair aside and nestled his nose into my neck. We cuddled for a moment, the memories of last night replaying in my mind, until we were interrupted by his phone ringing.

"Urgh," he groaned, "it's the partner." He sat up on the bed, cleared his throat and answered the phone, walking naked down the hall as he was talking, his voice fading away.

Gary and I stayed up all night, everything quickly escalating after we both finished a second bottle of wine. I thought he was going to kiss me goodnight, but he picked me up and pressed me against the wall, the passion I felt in Hawaii quickly, and naturally, reignited. He laid me on the dining table and went straight for my dessert making sure I orgasmed before filling me with himself. We moved to the couch and finally my bedroom. It was unexpected, but welcome, and I would say the wine and the beer got the better of us. I was glad it broke the ice between us though, as I couldn't have imagined sleeping in separate rooms, if I was being entirely honestly with myself.

He walked back in the room with an air of frustration, his hair messed in different directions. My eyes were drawn to his bare body, the way his chest hair slightly curled and the way the sunlight played on the contours of his muscles. They had asked him to inspect the site and he asked me to join him.

"Are you sure? Did you want your first meeting with them to be alone?" I asked. Gary shrugged.

"To be honest, I haven't got my bearings yet so if you came with me, it would be helpful. I haven't driven on the other side of the road yet either, you might want to ease me into it," he said, as I continued to lay in bed, the sheets wrapped around my bare body hoping he would lay back down next to me. He didn't. He went to his room to start getting ready. I listened to him unzip his suitcase and rummage through a few things. I heard clothes moving around the place, the shower turning on, and then watched him as he walked in again, almost exactly how I met him, with his jeans, white singlet and flannel overshirt.

"That attire? Do you need to be more big shot New York now?" I asked, being serious, but I think his exaggerated laugh meant he thought I was joking.

"C'mon, up. Let's go. I'll make you breakfast," he said, throwing at me the clothes he wore last night to bed. I liked this dynamic. It felt easy, it felt playful. It was something I hadn't experienced before.

The smell of coffee wafted through the kitchen corridor as I was walking closer to it. I watched Gary plate our breakfast up, the kitchen towel slung across his shoulder as he did at the pub, his brown beard neatly trimmed for the first time. Usually he went for a rougher, shaggier look. *Was it to impress me, or the restaurant guys?* He gestured for me to sit down this time like I had last night for him, and then plated the food and put the coffee in front of me, kissing me on the cheek as I thanked him. He made us bacon and eggs on toast, but it had a cafe flair to it; the way he grilled the tomatoes and the bread on the stove instead of putting it in the toaster.

"No-one has ever done this for me before, thank you," I said, thinking back to the boys from the Margaret River trip, which was the only time, but it wasn't solely for me.

"There's more where this came from, princess," he said with a wink, a playful smile spread across his face. He shared his nervousness for meeting the businessmen again, here in New York, and concerns about potential delays.

"I'm happy to give any financial tips. It's been a little while since I've flexed my finance muscle, but it's my bread and butter. If you need it, please ask," I said, as we started clearing the table.

By the time we arrived at the restaurant in the heart of central New York, the store front taped up from the inside with butchers paper so you couldn't see inside, there were about five men there, waiting for Gary. He did quick introductions and then began walking toward the kitchen to talk to the chef. I lingered in the foyer area, taking in the amount of money invested into the establishment. The entry had large real plants by the front with a black carpet that took you to a seated area where patrons could enjoy a drink while waiting for their table. The high ceilings with tall slim lights dropping about twenty feet with a warm glow pouring out of the globes. The tables and chairs were black, with longer tables along the sides and smaller tables near the entrance. The kitchen was behind glass, the room filled with stainless steel appliances. It was stunning. I could see the vision.

I went back to the car to grab an older camera I kept in there and began taking photos, capturing the elegance of the space. I then made my way to Gary, taking photos of him and everyone focusing on their given tasks.

"Are you a photographer?" one of the businessmen asked. He was a short, stout, older man, with a tailored crispy suit. "You can't share that publicly yet, we have a PR team for that," he said, an arrogance in his voice lifting.

"I'm a photographer yes, but I'm also Gary's housemate. Could I put together a bit of an article with the pictures and send it to you?" I asked, thinking proactively. I felt I knew the words to describe the success this could be. He nodded reluctantly, almost annoyed, and gave me his card. "This place is beautiful. I understand why Gary came here," I said, partly wanting to win him over, attending to his ego.

"It's going to take off, we already know that, but we want it good from the get-go," he said. "No room for error." I wondered the toll this would take on Gary and the fact he had risked his comfortable life in Scotland for the hustle and bustle of a busy restaurant in New York. I looked back at him, through the glass windows, talking to multiple people. He looked focused. He looked inspired. *I wonder how this will all play out for us?* When Gary was finished, a couple of hours later, I checked in on how he was feeling. While he seemed to be coordinating things well, I knew this was out of his comfort zone by the way his eyebrows furrowed, and his shoulders were slightly raised.

"I'm fine. That guy you were chatting to is a bit of a prick, but he knows his stuff," Gary said, a beer in his hand. We had strolled through the neighborhood and found a local bar to eat lunch. He told me there was conflict with the menus and what the chef wanted to do but didn't have the budget for. He shared that while he had managed the bar in Scotland, and knew it inside out, there was a big difference between a casual pub and this kind of restaurant. "We will work it out though," he said positively.

I told him how I was going to send through the photos I had taken and write up an article.

"I want to see if I can get into some kind of writing, to expand from photography now. I know it so well," I said, putting the idea out into the universe.

"That's a great idea, surely there are more opportunities here as well?" he said. I loved he was so supportive of my ideas.

"You know I told the prick guy I was your housemate?" I said, as our drinks arrived. I side-eyed him, a cheeky grin on my face, wanting to know what he had to say about it. He pulled me closer to him, his gaze locking into mine with a softening in his eyes.

"You're definitely not just a housemate to me. If you want to make things official, I'm ready" he said confidently as he kissed me.

"I'm ready too," I said, goosebumps crawling around my entire body. *Maybe this is our happy ending after all?*

44

Chance

Gary felt comfortable going to meet with the team himself as the days and weeks flew by and I was able to continue with getting the house ready and getting prints online for sale. I went through all the India and Australia images, picking out my favorite ones, editing them and adding them to my website. I sent a few to John, and Christian as well, as he had previously been in touch with artists who had purchased my prints to paint them. Sel had also become the ultimate wing woman at the art gallery, making sure everyone that walked through looked at my work and left with my business card – something I never felt confidence to do.

Business had picked up over the weeks too, and I had multiple photoshoots booked in from the one I did with Adeline. I also naturally fell into consulting with creatives, with John sharing what a great job I did with his art gallery. I had other galleries around the country asking me to assist them remotely.

I began submitting written articles for online and print travel magazines nationally, some were paid and some were unpaid, but I still took it as a win to practice this new venture of mine. I found a love for words and it made me think back to when I was in primary school and how I loved to read and write. It was a pattern I had come to notice, that I had always done what I loved doing – but the world got in the way as I grew older.

Looking at the pictures from when I was at the restaurant with Gary and the prick guy, who I found out was named Colin, I began writing the article for the restaurant launch. I talked about the unique architecture, the designer furniture and the high-profile names involved with the launch of the establishment. I talked about how it was already booked out for six months by celebrities and influencers and I was able to share a glimpse of the new menu and the unique ingredients coming from all around the world, along with photos Gary let me take during an exclusive invite-only tasting event he invited me to.

"I love it," Gary said proudly after he read it, "you need to do more of this, you're so good at it, Katie." It was the re assurance I needed to keep going and find the courage to press send.

I emailed it to Colin, also emailing a few photos of mine I had taken, imposing them onto an image of the restaurant wall. There was one image from the Australian trip at a Margaret River winery where the sun was setting and the glow of the sunset reflected magically against the rows of grapevines. The warm hues of the image perfectly enhancing the black and brass interior of the restaurant, amplifying the elegance that a bare wall wouldn't have been able to do. It was three pm the next afternoon when Colin responded with; Love it, we will order that print, if you can do it in the size you marked in the email. Thanks, C.

In the very same minute I saw the email, I ordered the print. Done, delivery will be in three days. I'll bring it with Gary, I wrote to him. He didn't mention anything about the article, but I still classed it as a win too.

45

Surprise

On the lead-up to the opening night. Colin officially reached out and told me they had used my article. They had barely changed it, using my images and my name, which gave me the credit I needed to increase my social media following, ultimately resulting in more booked photography sessions and article opportunities. There was an interest in my image on the wall, which was also posted on social media, and the enquiries came through to order the same print. Everyone wanted it.

Given Gary had to work for the opening, Adeline was my guest. We were seated with the corporates and their partners, however after introducing myself at the beginning and giving out my card, we were happy to keep quiet and to ourselves.

I quickly noticed that Adeline had taken photos with her champagne but hadn't had a sip. When the server came around to pour the red wine with the entrees, she also shook her head, this time looking at me.

"Are you joking?" I asked, my mouth dropping open with excitement without getting a response from her. She didn't need to say anything, the way her cheeks blushed pink and grinned was all I needed to know. I got up from my seat to reach over and hug her, squeezing her tight.

"It just happened, we weren't even trying. We were going to wait until next year."

"I am so glad I am back for this," I said, starting to cry with joy, knowing I wasn't going to miss such a milestone for my best friend. "How far along are you?"

"Only a few weeks, maybe six I think, so it's still early days, but I just have a good feeling, Katie."

"I'm going to be an aunty," I cried, my hand reaching across the table to hold her arm, not wanting to let her go.

"What's going on with you and Gary by the way?" Ads asked, to which I responded with a giddy smile.

"We seem to be going really well but I know this launch was a lot of pressure. There is a part of me that's worried this will be like Mark all over again. I don't see how he's going to get any flexibility here. Look at this place, it's packed." I said, looking toward the crowd of people eating their entrees, staff maneuvering between people; multiple waiters, about ten chefs in the kitchen, where we could see the high pressure through the glass window. Adeline could see what I meant. "I can't do that again. But look, who knows. He's been amazing, he's so thoughtful and kind and always makes time for us. He still makes me breakfast every morning. We will talk after this excitement settles down though."

"Are you two able to go on dates?" she enquired more. I know she was worried I wasn't getting the most out of a new relationship.

"Yes, we are, only like once a week. It's been a bit hard. And yes, the sex is still amazing, but let's see how sustainable it is with these work hours he's doing."

"Girl, I think he's smitten," Ads raised an eyebrow. I knew too. The way he made me coffee and put it on my bedside table before he left for the restaurant. The way he would call me first when there was exciting news about the restaurant. The way he would come back from a long day and still sit next to me and ask how my day was. And, oh, the way he supported me with my writing.

The night continued on impeccably, Colin standing for speeches and explaining the new technology they had adopted.

"When making the booking, you enter favorite drink and five minutes before your arrival time it will alert the staff. Then when you enter the venue, we use facial recognition to seat you at a specific seat in the waiting corner, and your drink will arrive." There were cheers erupting from the venue.

This was followed by the head chef explaining each course we had eaten and what was about to be served. After the main, Colin and Gary thanked everyone for attending.

"And I would like to thank my partner, Katie, for being incredibly supportive in the lead-up to the opening. I couldn't have done this without you, babe." There was a round of applause and he winked at me, his eyes filled with pride. Ads cheered with everyone else, pointing frantically at me, my face blushing deeply, overwhelmed.

Once dessert had been served and final speeches were said, everyone slowly left, including the corporates at our table. Adeline and I stayed, wanting to chat with Gary and the team after, knowing that's when the real celebration started.

"How do you think it went?" Gary asked, approaching us as the last person exited and the door had been locked.

"It was amazing, congratulations," I said, leaning in for a kiss, "and partner, hey? Never heard you use that word before," I teased.

"I had to thank you. It has been easier with you by my side and God, I love you," he said, grabbing my hand and pulling me close to him. I turned to Ads grinning.

"I love you too," I responded, the words escaping my mouth so easily, like they were always sitting there ready to be said.

He gestured to the barmen to bring a round of drinks.

"Not for me thanks," Ads quickly said, and I raised my eyebrows at Gary.

"Congratulations to you!" he reached in for a hug, "I'm looking forward to meeting Dan. Now that this is all done, I really hope it will settle down a little." I looked at Ads, sharing the same sentiment.

I left with Adeline, knowing Gary wanted to party with his team. He deserved to.

"Could we stop at the chemist on the way home?" I asked Ads, her face slowly turning toward me curiously, trying to read my face.

"Wait. Did you not drink alcohol for me, or for another reason?" she asked, seemingly like a joke.

"No, look, I don't know, I'm a bit late but I'm sure it's fine," I said, not being able to hide the concern.

"Are you two using protection?" she asked. I shook my head sideways … no.

"Gary knows I've been off contraception since Mark and I broke up and was timing our sex with my cycle but with all that's been going on with business and the opening I didn't realize until you told me you're pregnant that I haven't had a period for the entire time he's been here. It's been six weeks. I put it down to moving back and stress. I'm sure it's nothing."

"Let me know how it goes," Ads said as she dropped me off to my front door. "Do you want me to stay?" I shook my head, knowing it was late and we were both tired. I went straight to the bathroom, peed on the stick and sat there with my timer on.

I texted Adeline three minutes later: *Fuck. It's positive. What do I do?*

Acknowledgements

In the words of Olympic treasure Snoop Dogg, "I wanna thank me." The idea of this trilogy has been in the works since 2013, however I knew I needed to grow into who I am now to be write about it.

The original book *Dancing Skies & City Lights* was borne from the support of so many, while this book was created during one of the most difficult phases of my life where it burned to the ground, only to rebuild into something more beautiful than I could have ever imagined. Things that got me through and learned along the way, are scattered throughout this.

I would like to thank one of my best friends, Tegan. It was so enjoyable sharing this editing journey with you, and how invested you are in Kate's journey – and mine too. It's an honour to have you by my side in this life.

And thank you to Johnny, for being my Gary.

To all my readers, I am so grateful for you following this journey … the last book to this trilogy will be a big one!

About the Author

Sheleila is the author of *Dancing Skies & City Lights*, *Strayed Love* and children's book *The Quacking Frog*. She is also a co-author in three non-fiction anthologies, *The FIFO Wives' Tales*, *Love, Bruises & Bullsh!t* and *Hear Us Roar: Lioness Edition*.

Sheleila draws inspiration in her writing through her own experiences – travelling to thirty-three countries at the time of publishing. She has backpacked her way through Asia and Europe, couch-surfed from Scotland to England while touring on a $300 (£150) second-hand bicycle and also reconnected with estranged family while living in Canada.

A world traveller, people lover and experience seeker   it's her mission to inspire people to move past their comfort zone.

Sheleila D'Paiva

'Whether you think you can, or you think you can't – you're right.'
– Henry Ford

www.sheleila.com.au

@sheleiladp.author
Sheleila D'Paiva – Author
Sheleila D'Paiva

Other Works

Dancing Skies & City Lights has won a silver Literary Titan book award in 2023 and won a silver for the Bookfest Fall Awards 2023.

Love Bruises & Bullshit sharing stories on domestic violence experience in Australia, won a gold ABLE Golden book award in 2024 and a gold Literary Titan book award in 2022.

The FIFO Wives' Tales, creating discussion on the fly-in fly-out lifestyle, won a gold Literary Titan book award in 2022 and is a number-one Amazon bestseller.

The Quacking Frog